# THE ANGEL'S BACKBONE

THE PREQUEL

# The Angel's Backbone

## A SEASON OF EFFECTUATION

### DAVID C. HASCALL

LUMINARE PRESS

WWW.LUMINAREPRESS.COM

The Angel's Backbone
© 2019 by David C. Hascall

Printed in the United States of America

Cover Design: Claire Flint Last
Map by EncMstr - Own work, CC BY-SA 3.0,
https://commons.wikimedia.org/w/index.php?curid=2956010

Luminare Press
442 Charnelton
Eugene, OR 97401
www.luminarepress.com

LCCN: 2019916325
ISBN: 978-1-64388-240-6

*For my mother, Kathleen Alice Hascall, who, as a new bride, followed her dream west. You tended my many wounds, with never a complaint.*

*Also for the unknown pioneer woman buried along the historic Barlow Road in the shadow of Mount Hood. You came so close to your dream.*

# Contents

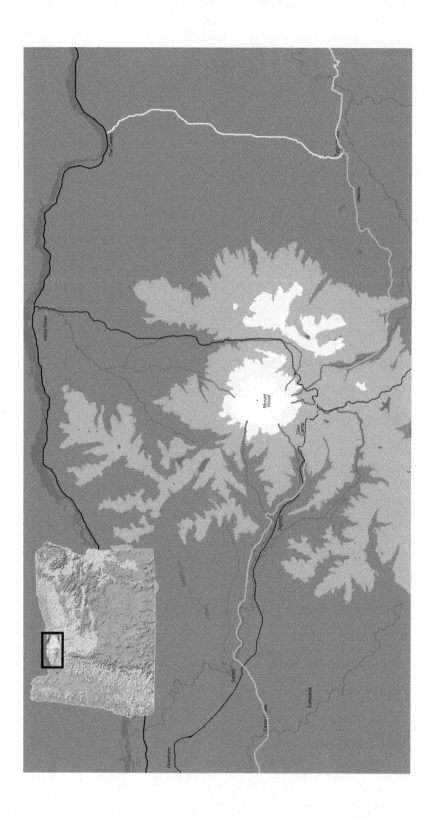

*The construction of the Barlow Road contributed more towards the prosperity of the Willamette Valley and the future State of Oregon, than any other achieve'ment prior to the building of the railways in 1870."*

—MATTHEW DEADY,
Oregon's first federal judge

# Preface

THIS NOVEL IS A WORK OF HISTORICAL FICTION SET IN THE year 1869. It serves as a prequel to my earlier works. The Rainbow Roads Trilogy follows in time *The Longest Wooden Railroad, 1929, Tahoe of the North, 1939,* and *The Color of Shadows, 1949.* It traces the roots of Verin Palmer, also known as Virgil Stubbs, patriarch of a pioneer family who settled in Horton, Oregon. He was said to have walked barefoot across the prairie.

His journey west is not the central focus here; rather, *The Angel's Backbone* highlights the beginning and the end of his travels, as he experiences them in the company of trusted friends, and explores how these persons chose to start and finish their journeys, making fateful decisions, and taking risks.

The historical events that influenced each person to choose to go west might not strike the reader as the typical ones. Traveling the final one hundred miles, known to be the most difficult along the Oregon Trail, rarely receives the notoriety it deserves. At the time, it meant choosing between treacherous Barlow Road, which was the first land route through the Cascade Mountains, or rafting down the Columbia River. Travelers paid dearly for their choices in hard currency and sometimes with their lives.

By 1869, more than thirty years had passed since the first wave of missionaries surged west to Oregon. Jason Lee, the first missionary to minister to the Willamette Valley, arrived in 1834. There is evidence that his interest followed an inquiry by the Nez Perce Indians, who were looking for the so-called "Book of Heaven."

On his return to the east to gather support for another trip, Lee went on tours, describing the importance of spreading the gospel of Christianity to the Native American peoples *first*, and emphasizing the value of white colonization of the Oregon Territory. "A few good, pious settlers would benefit generations yet unborn," he proclaimed.

Doctor Marcus Whitman helped lead the first wagon train to Oregon in 1836, led another in 1842, and established a mission for the Cayuse and Flat Head Indians near Walla Walla, Washington.

Adventurers rushed to take advantage of the offering of free land in the Oregon Territory in 1843, and to California when gold was discovered there in 1849. The hardships and rewards of following different routes overland, or of sailing around South America, filled diaries and made newspaper headlines for years.

Homestead Acts passed by Congress in 1862, 1873, 1904, 1909, and 1916 allowed for the creation of small dry land farms all across the mid-west. A rising tide of immigrant farmers turned to a flood that continued for the next century.

Former Union soldiers, exempt from improving the land to establish a dry land claim, leapfrogged farther and farther west, abandoning smaller acreages for larger ones with better soil and more abundant water.

The largest redistribution of the American population in our nation's history was well underway by 1869. In places, the westward trail widened to twenty miles to accommodate so many wagons traveling the same route at the same time! Immigrants from Europe and Asia also joined the race for free land, and many were granted citizenship in the process.

Within the space of a few years, more than five hundred thousand men, women, and children left relative security in the east to start a new life in the west. The opportunity of a lifetime was waiting, if they could just get there. Factors influencing the decisions to head west included the Civil War and its aftermath, Reconstruction, and attempts to escape the waves of infectious diseases that swept through the east: scarlet fever in 1865, cholera in 1866, and periodic outbreaks of endemic tuberculosis.

Rather than avoiding catastrophe, they found others along the trail. Food poisoning, water-borne diseases, gunshot wounds, and snakebites took the lives of more than twenty-three thousand pioneers: a grave along the trail every eighty yards for more than two thousand miles!

Of those who did arrive overland at The Dalles, along the banks of the mighty Columbia River, some travelers were too ill or too exhausted to continue the journey. The Cascade Mountains and eleven-thousand-foot-high Mount Hood presented nearly impassable barriers.

For those pioneers who chose a raft trip down the river through treacherous rapids as their last leg of the journey, their sense of wonder was perhaps renewed by seeing some one hundred scenic waterfalls that spilled over the canyon walls into the river, by the pristine forests, and by the panoramic view of the deep gorge itself.

Why didn't the author's group of travelers wait one more month for the completion of the Transcontinental Railroad, achieved in May of 1869? That railroad's seven-year construction period would certainly have been widely publicized. The overland journey could then have been made in relative comfort, and the trip shortened from six months to six days!

The fledgling network of communities built to serve the wagon roads withered in the face of the railroads, as new towns sprang up along the rails. America was open for business coast to coast, thanks to that iron network. Long after the best land had been claimed, the rivers polluted, and the gold fields exhausted, the siren song continued, and was perhaps overstated, to keep people moving west.

Today, 20/20 hindsight makes us shake our heads at what seems to be unnecessary sacrifice; however, those who traveled across country in 1869 must have measured the risks —or perhaps they did not.

To honor the pioneers who courageously persevered to accomplish their dreams regardless of the sacrifices, and to acknowledge making such difficult choices as those required at the beginning and end of the journey, with the outcome uncertain, this book has been written. For them it was *A Season of Effectuation*.

**Effectuation** (noun): The act of beginning and carrying through to completion. Per American Heritage Roget's Thesaurus, the effectuation principle in action is opportunity identification in situations of uncertainty in which the future is unpredictable, goals are not clearly defined, and there is no ultimate selection mechanism.

# Prologue

*October 10 1869*

AN UNUSUALLY STRONG WEST WIND, KNOWN AS A 'CHINOOK' to the Native American people of the Columbia River Basin, swept inland from the Pacific Ocean and funneled into the Columbia River Gorge. Bringing a torrential downpour, it drenched the west-facing windward side of Mount Hood with six inches of rain, and dumped more than a foot of snow on the leeward side.

When the skies cleared, the highest peak in Oregon showed white for a hundred miles.

Denied by the mountains, the wind sped inland, using the Columbia River as its highway. Forced through the Narrows, and up over Celilo Falls, it followed the river north, twisting like the slither of a sidewinding rattlesnake. It spread out over the river's lower banks and blew across the rolling hills of the Palouse Country until it butted heads like a Billy goat against the Bitterroot Mountains of western Idaho. In a relentless quest to be free, it followed the Snake and Clearwater Rivers south, then east. It twisted and turned through Hell's Canyon, the deepest river gorge in North America, unyielding to travelers, and bitterly cold to every living thing.

It broke through the Rocky Mountains at South Pass, the pioneer's gateway to the west, and spread out across the deserts of the Great Basin. Without deference or remorse, it suddenly disappeared, swallowed whole by the unexpected expanse of openness.

If it had become a living thing along the way, perhaps capable of remorse, one that deserved justice for such an abrupt and rude demise, no creature who suffered its effect would have granted it anything, or wept as it passed away. Indifference toward soulless things is natural.

# PART I

October 11 1869

# CHAPTER 1

# The Empty Holster

THE POWERFUL, RELENTLESS WIND FELT LIKE A LIVING THING to Virgil Stubbs as it blew inland up the Columbia Gorge and swept over him as he climbed the hill above The Dalles. If it had been something that could be struck, the eighteen-year-old would have pulled off his coat and gloves, exposing his arms and bare knuckles, and swung both fists at it. His hands were unusually large for his age, but not from fighting. He had assumed the task of milking a Jersey cow to earn his supper, shortly after leaving Independence, at the start of the long journey west. His formerly scrawny arms and hands had strengthened rapidly.

He had never been good with letters and numbers, but he learned plenty about some of life's other important lessons. *Don't fall in love with no older woman. No point goin' further west. No point in anything a'tall.* His brown eyes were slits against the wind, damming the flow of tears that streaked his leathery sunburnt face. A nagging toothache came to life every time he opened his mouth to take a breath.

Working his way farther uphill above the Columbia River, he felt the tremendous power of the wind at his back. It pushed him forward against his will. If he turned to face into it and tried to resist, it landed punch after punch, the way a skilled prizefighter would; it pummeled him, searching for a decisive opening to knock the boy down.

Oregon was a different destination than what he had envisioned; there was no denying it any longer. It had become a place of shattered dreams—a place of hardship and death.

What lay ahead for Virgil was something unimaginable for anyone less weary, of any age, who hadn't walked the miles he had in bare feet. His destination was the Mount Hood Pioneer Cemetery, where he was to dig two graves.

Weighed down by his thoughts as well as a shovel, he reflected that he would have preferred that a hungry wolf chase him uphill, rather than the wind. The wolf would nip at his heals, toy and tire him to exhaustion, then make the kill swiftly with its powerful jaws.

The bone-chilling wind had made its way inside his heavy coat, entering through the threadbare spaces at both elbows. It inflated like a balloon. The collar slapped his bare face, stinging the end of his nose like a yellow jacket.

His cold feet were calloused from walking the two thousand miles from Independence, Missouri. He had never thought much about protecting them, until now. He could easily have fashioned moccasins from the empty leather holster he had found after leaving Fort Hall. It lay in a wagon wheel rut carved deeply into the rock: When metal-shrouded wagon wheel met solid rock, metal had always won.

The holster now hung heavy at his waist, a symbol of defeat—a reminder of her, of Claire O' Connor.

He had had a special plan for the holster, a dream that kept him going day after day, mile after mile. He intended to make it a gift to her on his birthday, the same day he planned to propose.

*Th' last hunnert miles over th' Barlow Road to th' Willamette Valley're sposed t' be th' hardest, but we'll be stronger, her 'n me together*, he thought. In preparation for his proposal, he carved their initials in the leather, and then filled the holster with wild desert flowers when they crossed the Snake River at Farewell Bend. The flowers had quickly withered, been replaced, and withered again in the hot desert sun. Since her refusal, his life seemed to wither, too.

Virgil sighed heavily. The empty holster could have only one use now. If he lived long enough, he intended to acquire a revolver, perhaps a Schofield, like the one carried by his Uncle Stubbs. He would protect it with the sturdily-crafted holster.

He trudged over the last few yards toward the burial plots, holding on to the wrought iron fence that surrounded the cemetery for balance, using his other hand to keep his battered hat on his head. Unsure how to manage with the shovel he carried, he pitched it over the fence. The wind caught it and it flew through the air, glanced off a headstone, and landed some distance away.

The Mount Hood Pioneer Cemetery gate hung open, poorly supported by a single rusting hinge. It rested on the dirt as if, like the people buried here, it too relied on the soil to give relief from the suffering and the signs of obvious decay.

The other two hinges had shared the weight of the gate initially, just as camaraderie had supported the pioneers when they started their journey across the Oregon Trail. Most wagon trains arriving from the east had had to make their ways uphill, during their brief stays in the area, to deposit their dead. The gate had swung to and fro repeatedly until it wore out; an over-used revolving door. Two of the three hinges eventually broke free, fell away, and disappeared in the dirt. Man met nature, but this time nature won.

Virgil pushed against the gate. It squealed loudly, fighting him. Only when he lifted it high enough to clear the weeds could he pull it open.

Inside the fenced enclosure, the raised mounds were hardly distinguishable from the grass, weeds, and rocks. Not all the graves were marked with stone or wooden crosses. Evidently, no one was around to do perpetual care, as was the common practice back east. *Mebbe dead folks're just left alone here*, Virgil thought.

He retrieved the shovel and looked for a suitable site. No one was there to tell him where to dig, and as he surveyed the grounds for a place big enough for two graves, he thought: *This job's gonna be a toughie.*

He pulled his wide-brimmed hat down hard over his brow, and pulled the collar of his heavy winter coat higher and tighter around his face. He gazed at the desolate landscape. *I couldn't never live in no place like this. The further west I go, th' less there is...fewer th' reasons to've come here.*

He was more upset with himself than with Claire. He had misunderstood her feelings toward him. *She said no to me, no marriage, simple as that.*

"Better git a move on, Virgil. Time's a-wastin,'" he said out loud. He knew the Reverend Donald Ricketts would perform a brief funeral service at ten o'clock. *He's done a-plenty of 'em before— I lost count at forty.*

*I don't know the whole story of them that I'm doing th' diggin' for. We was all sick an' tuckered out when we got here, fourteen wagons left of thirty-five that left th' Mississippi River six months ago.*

He stood for a moment, wondering if the site he had chosen had been passed over for a reason by other gravediggers, then removed his coat, flung it carelessly on the ground, and got to work. For the next hour, he thought only about the size of the holes and not about Claire O'Connor.

He stopped to rest, perspiring heavily, when the first hole was nearly finished. He wiped his parched lips. *I didn't bring no water.*

He looked, for the first time, at the names written on nearby graves, some chiseled into stone, others hastily carved into weathered strips of wood. *Their stories're same as ours, I betcha. Wonder if their pullin' stock was divided up, like Cap'n Stubbs did of them that died with us. Made sense to beef up th' weaker wagon teams—long as we didn't mix mules with horses, and b'sides, what else was we s'posed to do with th' cattle?*

He stared into the open hole he had dug, wondering what his uncle would say if it wasn't right. He decided to step off the length. Placing one foot in front of the other, he counted six paces. He was satisfied. *Same's me. Dig one hole my size, a little more'n six feet. That's what Uncle Stubbs said. T'other one's for th' wife, she's a small one. Five feet long, mebbe.*

His uncle, Rufus Stubbs, was the wagon master. *He sent me to do the diggin'. No matter that today's m' birthday.*

Not wanting to dwell on thoughts of how he had intended to celebrate the day, Virgil paused to remember the deceased man and his wife. *Verin an' 'Lizabeth Palmer were th' same age, thirty-eight.* The circumstances of Verin Palmer's death no longer felt out of the ordinary to Virgil.

*After his wife died, he shot hisself rather'n go on alone. They come all this way. Hunnert miles t' go an' both come up short. Mebbe lookin' at the snow was what done it. They was from the south somewheres, like me an' Uncle Stubbs. Mebbe they didn't never see snow b'fore. I hadn't.*

Elizabeth's death had not been unexpected. *She died from drinkin' bad water outten a creek that runned into th' Snake; suffered stomach trouble for more'n a month. She shoulda knowed better.*

He looked back down the hill toward the Columbia River, and remembered the lack of excitement four days earlier, when the travelers in the Stubbs party saw Celilo Falls for the first time.

*We had t' pay fer a place t' camp along th' riverbank. Dozens of wagons ahead of us. Some of 'em had been lined up and waitin' more'n a week. No rafts handy to take 'em on down th' river.*

Thoughts of Claire flooded over him again. *She wanted to float on down. I didn't, but I'da gone along, did what she wanted. We was to be married, I was sure. I had plans. But her words, she didn't care how they come out. Seven years. Seven years diff'rence, she kept sayin'.*

"What diff'rence does seven years make out here anyways!" he shouted at her. "How kin you say no? Today's my birthday! It'll be our anniversary, 'n we'll have plenty to celebrate!"

Virgil picked up the shovel to start digging the second grave, but threw it back down. He longed to rush back to her wagon and plead with her to reconsider. *She needs a man, she's alone too, her folks died weeks ago.*

Unwelcome tears stung his cheeks. *She cut me deeper'n this cussed wind.*

Anger boiled to the surface, almost displacing his grief. He swung his fist at the air. His shoulders shaking with despair, eyes burning, he tried to blink away the pain, wiping his face with the back of his sleeve. He stared again at the open hole in the ground. *Just my size. I got nothin'. I got nobody. I got nothin' to leave to nobody, 'cept the holster, an' it ain't worth nothin'.*

*I picked a passel of flowers, the day 'fore we got here, an' packed dirt around the stems an' roots—lavender colored sage, and some other li'l pink an' yeller posies—no idea what them're called. She rejected them, too! An' here I was, thinkin' it was the perfect time an' place to ask 'er for her hand.*

He had beamed at her expectantly, eager as a schoolboy, but her expression changed. *She started a-shakin' her head, an' handed it all back, when she saw our initials,* **VS loves CO,** *carved on th' back of th' holster.*

"Virgil, I'm seven years old than you. I need to marry an older man. What would people say? If my folks were still alive, what would they say?"

Shocked and surprised, he had no answer. He walked hastily away from her, confused and hurt, and dumped on the ground the flowers he had so carefully and lovingly arranged. *Mebbe I shoulda spent more time lookin' fer a Schofield revolver, just like Uncle Stubbs carries.*

He unbuckled the holster belt and looked at the initials he had carved. He had been so careful, getting the letters even. *She'll never see 'em again.* His face was streaked with salty sweat mixed with tears that had washed away only a small amount of the grime that had caked on his face. Virgil knew that his pain would be more difficult to wash away. He mockingly mimicked her words: "What would people say?"

*That holster fell out the back o' someone's wagon. I run up th' line, askin' each family, were it theirs. Nobody claimed it. Mebbe if it held a pistol then, somebody woulda taken it. If it held one now, mebbe I'd use it.*

The thought of killing himself had never before occurred to him. With shocking clarity, he realized he was contemplating suicide. *It'll satisfy. I c'n end th' pain 'n fergit th' disappointment. No point in goin' on. We made so many stops on th' way here t' bury our dead. What's one more man with big ideas, like these other folks buried all around, joinin' 'em in the ground t' be forgotten?*

*There was that family at the river here, shoutin' at each other, the day we got here. They were next in line fer a raft—one was*

14

*comin' the next day, someone told 'em. Two of 'em were in a tug-a-war, fightin' over a wooden bucket. They'd been told to lighten the load on th' raft an' couldn't agree on how to do it. They gived up their place in line to sort it out. Even a bucket meant somethin' 'til it got here. Everything had a use—a future—'til we come here to face that mountain. Capt'n Stubbs woulda dealt with them two. He woulda said, "If you cain't keep up, lighten the load on the stock, or I'll do it for y'all!"*

Virgil realized that an occasional word delivered with an unmistakable southern accent still emerged from both his uncle and himself, Georgia natives, although they had worked hard at getting rid of it. Many of the travelers in the Stubbs wagon party were Yankees, and prejudiced against southerners.

Another surge of anger swept over him, just as a sudden gust of wind threatened to blow the hat off his head. *If only I had the Cap'n's pistol now, I c'd end it all an' let someone else do the diggin'—just close the grave over me.*

He threw the holster as far as he could. Carried by the wind, it sailed through the air, landed against the cemetery fence, and hung there like a crucifix.

On impulse, Virgil laid down in the open grave. He stretched out on his back and crossed his arms, the way he had seen the dead placed before they were wrapped in a blanket and buried, time and time again, all the way across the prairie. He closed his eyes and tried to imagine what dying would feel like.

He laid the shovel by his right side and wrapped his arm around it, almost as if embracing a loved one.

His heart was beating rapidly. He could feel it throbbing in his neck and wondered what it would take to make it stop. *Stop all th' pain—then all th' memories of Claire'll be gone. Stop my heart. Stop m' life. I'll be at peace here along with th' rest o' these folks.*

He closed his eyes and pulled his bandana up, covering his nose and mouth. He yanked his floppy sweat-stained hat down to cover his forehead and eyes. Everything was dark.

The persistent wind gusted across the open grave. Loose soil and small rocks tumbled in on top of him. His muslin shirt and bib trousers were soon dusted with a thin layer of the rocky soil.

His hands still ached from the dig, and his old leather gloves had worn through in several places. He flexed his fingers, ripped off the gloves, and threw them over the dirt pile. *Worthless like me!*

Virgil let himself sob loudly, and then howled like an angry baby, certain that no one was nearby, that he could not be heard. "Mebbe a man sh'd just choose th' day he dies!" he shouted to the skies above. His sobs turned to whimpers before he fell silent.

"Don't I look good now." The words escaped his lips as he lay there, words of comfort often shared by those wishing to make someone feel something besides revulsion when staring death in the face.

To anyone grieving over him, a gifted mortician might have received the credit for the rouge upon his cheeks, but the rosy complexion came from one sunburn after another as he had crossed the prairie. The color never seemed to completely peel away or tan before his skin reddened again.

His tears cascaded down the edges of his eyes and dripped steadily into the cold soil, like the Oregon rain, but not enough to quench the thirsty desert ground beneath him.

He grasped the shovel with both hands and struggled, from his prone position, to fill it. He dumped half a scoop of the rocky soil onto his feet. *If only I had a pistol 'stead of a shovel.* He felt warm. The grave provided a break from the wind, and the dirt, a comforting insulation. The sensation surprised him. After three tries, he was able to fill the shovel completely without disturbing the dirt on top of him. Once he got the knack, he filled the shovel and then dumped the contents over his legs, again and again, up to his waist.

He filled in the sides and leveled the mound he was building, not knowing why smoothing the edges seemed to matter to him. The dirt covered him from the chest down. It rose and fell with his breathing, and he was surprised and a little afraid of its weight.

He held his breath for as long as he could. Try though he might, his thoughts returned to Claire. *Did me bein' a southerner have somethin' to do with it? Mebbe she thought she'd do better with a northerner, since she's one herself. But I never shot no Yankee boys in the war!*

He looked at the cold gray sky through bloodshot eyes and yelled: "I don't care whether I live or die anymore. I don't care about you, Claire, or you, Uncle Stubbs!"

Except for his face and arms, Virgil's rail-thin body had disappeared in the open grave. He felt cramps in his feet, and considered lifting the dirt and wiggling free. *So, do I want to die, or don't I?* A little pain was nothing compared to the ache in his heart. A little pain would be a small price to pay to be free.

A shadow drifted over him. *A cloud bringin' in more damn' rain! What am I gonna do, lay here an' drown? If I'm gonna pull the dirt down over my face an' suffocate, it's time to just do it!* He struggled to fill the shovel one last time. He was unable to see the dirt that remained, but was determined to not disturb the earth that already covered him.

# CHAPTER 2

# A Melody of Peace

"JESUS, JOSEPH, AND MARY, VIRGIL! YOU SCARED THE LIVING daylights out of me!" resounded the voice of Reverend Donald Ricketts. "What are you doing down in that hole?"

Virgil stammered out: "Just measurin' the fit, Rev'rend."

"Well, you come up outta there, now!"

"A man sh'd choose th' day he dies; don't ya think, Rev'rend?"

Virgil tried to struggle to his feet. The Reverend reached down to help.

"God chooses that day, Virgil," he said as if beginning a well-rehearsed sermon to a packed sanctuary.

Reverend Ricketts was a strong man, and he pulled Virgil to his feet with ease. Stunned by what he had just witnessed, he clasped his long arms behind his back and strolled a few feet away, giving both of them a chance to collect themselves. His lengthy stride, long black coat and Padre hat had been, by design, his way to give reassurance to the weary. At the moment, however, the look on his chiseled features was closer to panic, and the scar on his forehead, always more noticeable when he was upset, throbbed a dark red.

"He's been choosin' regular like, ain't He? Don't seem right to me. Two more of our own dyin' here, after all we been through."

"A man lays in an open grave, that don't seem righteous to me," the reverend replied, turning back and regaining his composure. "You should beg forgiveness for your lack of faith."

Virgil had not envisioned trying to explain what he planned to do, or what the problem was. He tried to justify his attempt to kill himself in the rush of words he blurted out: "Claire won't miss me! She said as much! Serve her right to see me layin' here dead! Mister Palmer, he gave up for his own reasons, I got mine!"

"You're dying and wanting to punish Claire at the same time? What did she do, to deserve such wrath at the hands of another child of God?"

Virgil paused as he thought whether he should share the embarrassing truth. "Not marryin' me!" he announced. "She said no to it."

Reverend Ricketts nodded and picked up the shovel. "I see. I think you need a staff to lean on, Virgil, like this shovel. The staff of life is the Lord God above, just as here on earth, it's the wagon master. You want me to have a word with him?"

"Nah, Rev'rend. I'll do it."

"I come to help you with the digging then. Lots of rock in that dirt pile. This the only spot?"

Virgil nodded.

"Wagon's over yonder with the two to bury, the Palmers. That is, unless Scout there don't run on up the hill with the wagon— been nervous as a new bride lately," he said, then regretted his words. He quickly changed the subject. "Captain Stubbs is on his way up, got Claire on his arm. Some others are walking behind. Don't matter which direction we all go, does it? Captain Stubbs is always in the lead."

Virgil didn't answer.

The reverend turned to gaze west at snow-covered Mount Hood before he spoke again. *What can I tell this boy that will make a difference? I know what I interrupted. He was convincing himself that life isn't worth living.* Never good at thinking on his feet in a pinch, he plunged forward. "She's a-wearing that pretty dress, Claire is." He looked briefly at Virgil, hoping the boy didn't realize how inadequate he felt. "It's the white one that belonged to her mother."

Virgil stood next to him, looked down at the approaching party, took the shovel from the older man's hand, and began digging feverishly.

"Best not to keep a thing like this bottled up inside, Virgil. Being here, with that mountain standing there guarding the entry to the valley is doing strange things to people. Snow makes for a pretty scene on that mountain, just the same, don't you think?" *Distract and disarm.* "Those trees there," he pointed at the foothills, "the tops all covered in snow like that, remind me of a flock of sheep. It's a wolf in sheep's clothing for whoever goes near it now, they say."

He turned back toward Virgil. "You see a lot of snow down south?"

Virgil stopped digging and stiffened. "Not back home in Georgia, Rev'rend."

"Thought as much. You and the captain are kin to one another, aren't you?"

"We don't let on he's my uncle, on account o', y'all are Yankees," Virgil replied sarcastically.

Reverend Ricketts nodded, and turned his gaze north across the Columbia River. "I've been down south," he said, dreamily. "I was raised in Chicago, though. Hot in summer there, too. We both got a big river back home like this one, the Mississippi. I don't expect you care to ever see it again?"

Virgil continued to dig without comment. Ricketts took the shovel from him, speaking as he dug, while Virgil moved dirt and small rocks with his large, dirty hands.

"The Palmers will be side by side, overlooking them rolling hills on the other side of the river there, enjoying the peaceful view, never knowing what's on the other side. No more worries."

"She wants t' marry an older man, Rev'rend Ricketts," Virgil said sadly, kicking the dirt, some of which fell into the empty grave.

"Only God knows the future, Virgil. And it won't matter to you," he glanced briefly at the boy, "if you're lying down here all covered up. That's not what you really want, is it? To never see her again in that pretty dress? To never have another chance?"

"No, Rev'rend, I guess not."

*I have to tell him the real reason I came to the cemetery early before the others arrive. Before it's too late for both of them.*

"Can't say what your uncle would say about it all, either. Or what he might do, if you're not there to watch his back. Especially not now that there's trouble in the camp."

Virgil shifted his gaze from the open grave, which was almost deep enough, to Ricketts. "I ain't dead yet, Rev'rend. What trouble?"

"Most folks know about you two being from one of the former Confederate states. It never was a problem, 'til we got here. People overlook what they don't want to see when they're getting what they want. Once we came in sight of the mountain, after the captain said he couldn't decide which way to go from here, to get around it, people stopped being so forgiving of which side you two were on.

"There's a lot of blame flying around camp this morning, most of it pointed at the captain, for getting us here late in the season when the river is running full over the banks and the rafts can't get up this far. I came up early to tell you. It doesn't look good for either one of you."

"I done nothin' to nobody!" Virgil exclaimed defensively. "An' he ain't in charge of th' weather!"

"But they know you'll back any move he makes to save himself."

Virgil was thinking fast. "What am I gonna do, Rev'rend? Cap'n Stubbs is my only kin."

"My turn in the hole. Why don't you ask around here? Got to be better than a hundred people lying here who would say plenty if they could, about how unfair life is. Maybe some of them think they got a raw deal from the Almighty. And I'm sure some of them were from the south."

"They don't have nothin' to say no more," Virgil mumbled.

"But *you* do," Reverend Rickets countered, looking up at Virgil. "This grave is deep enough for Elizabeth." For the second time, he extended his hand to Virgil, who pulled hard to help the pastor out of the grave. "You need to warn your uncle. If he won't lead the wagons over the Barlow Road or help us get us through the rapids, they might try to hang the both of you."

"Mebbe me an' Cap'n Stubbs shoulda never come. An' you just said God chooses who lives an' who dies. Then why'd he make his decision early for alla these folks here that come west? Mebbe he didn't want 'em here. Like me, they done nothin' wrong."

"I don't know, Virgil. Lots of boys lying in the ground back east, too; the war made their decision for them. Most didn't know why they had to die. I saw it on both sides. I wrote a lot of letters home for them, mostly saying goodbye to somebody. There were so many… Sometimes, I'll admit, when I was tired, like I know we all were, I listened, and just pretended to write.

"Some of the folks in our train wouldn't risk going any farther 'til spring, anyway. I can't blame them. Dying in the last hundred miles isn't what I have in mind."

"Me neither, Rev'rend."

"What are you going to do, Virgil, after you warn the captain? Leaving looks like better odds than staying. What I saw when I came up here and looked down in this grave was a man ready to give up. You need to know more about life. You have a lot of growing up to do."

"If I'm a-gonna run, I gotta tell Claire good-bye to her face. I owe her that."

"Someday, God willing, if you're both still alive after we get to the Valley, why don't you ask her again?"

"I intend to. Let's put our backs to it, Rev. They're almost here."

Working together, the two men quickly finished digging the second grave.

Captain Stubbs lifted the gate all the way open, making room for several men to carry the bodies through the opening and into the graveyard. The gate's remaining hinge broke in the powerful grip of the wagon master. He threw the gate out of the way.

"You finished, Virgil?"

"Coupla' more minutes, Cap'n."

Reverend Ricketts waited for the people to form a circle around the graves. The wind blew steadily. Standing in the open, there was nothing they could do but endure it.

"Dearly beloved children of God, we are here today to bear witness to the loss of two of God's chosen people: Verin Carl Palmer and Elizabeth Rachel Palmer. If they were standing here with us, they would ask us not to weep for them, but to finish the journey we started six months ago!

"They accepted the challenges, and understood that all who start a race know that not everyone wins a ribbon, and not all finish. Yes, we carry the burden that they are not with us, but we are girded up with the strength given to us by their example." *That was a dumb thing to say*, he thought. *Palmer put a gun to his head.*

"Our burden is not... not made heavier by their death." He paused and swept his hand in a dramatic half-circle, pointing out the vista around the cemetery.

"Our captain has brought us to this beautiful place." He turned and looked squarely at Virgil. "Ours is not a decision about choosing life over death, but about choosing an honorable life of faith."

Virgil's eyes met Claire's. She was staring at him, mouthing the words for him to see: "I'm sorry." *I am so sorry that I have hurt you more than a thousand apologies can repair*, she thought.

Reverend Ricketts sang the words of a familiar hymn. When he got to the refrain, all present joined in:

*"We are gathered at the river, friends,*
*Where bright angel feet have trod,*
*With its crystal tide forever*
*Flowing by the throne of God."*

*Refrain:*

*"Yes, we'll gather at the river,*
*The beautiful, the beautiful river;*
*Gather with the saints at the river,*
*That flows by the throne of God."*

Reverend Ricketts raised his hand to quiet the gathering and spoke the final verse, changing several of the words:

*"Soon we'll reach the silver river, the Pacific Ocean.*
*Soon our pilgrimage will cease;*
*Soon our happy hearts will quiver*
*With the melody of peace."*

"Let us pray."

After the service, Captain Stubbs mingled with the mourners, consoling, comforting, and listening to the memories shared of the Palmers. He had pushed the couple multiple times to lighten the load on their stock of horses, and had lent a hand on many other tasks. He knew most of the stories already. Holding his hat on his head against the relentless breeze with one hand, shaking hands and patting shoulders with the other, he ended up next to his nephew, without losing sight of Claire, who stood with the others on the far side of the circle.

He put his hand on Virgil's shoulder and whispered in his ear. "Ask her to marry you again someday, son," he said. "You got nothing to lose. Just like the night we left Savannah." He offered a weary smile. "I need to come by your fire tonight. Build one away from the camp. We both need to look on down the trail, son."

In a resoundingly loud, cheerful voice, while clapping Virgil on the back, he then said: "Look at this beautiful morning! The rain goes and the sun comes out. It makes everything molasses sweet again! Virgil, you and Miss Claire take the wagon back on down to the camp, now that the Reverend's said his piece, just like we agreed." He winked at his nephew.

Neither of the young persons objected as he shepherded them out of the cemetery's enclosure. He helped Claire up to the seat while Virgil loosened the reins from the fence.

Virgil climbed up beside Claire, his heart pounding with fear and rejoicing at the nearness of her. The trip back to camp felt longer than the nearly two thousand miles Virgil had already traveled. Although a myriad of words and phrases swirled through his head, neither said a word until they reached the riverbank close to Claire's wagon.

She finally spoke, hesitating as she tried to find the words she sought. "I have to try and explain," she began. "Right now, it's hard, the funeral, I mean. It reminds me of losing my parents. Hearing the talk in camp, about the decisions we all have to make—it's just too much. You've been a good friend to me, and good to the oxen, Bess and Tillie. Come to eat supper with me. We can talk then. If you want to?"

Virgil nodded without speaking. Afraid of blurting out words that would sound awkward and childish, elated that he would have another chance to be near her, he hurried away.

Later that evening, after they had shared a companionable meal, eaten mostly in silence, Claire tried to lighten the mood. She commented on the dinner she had made for them. The sourdough bread, dried beef and corn meal was smothered with a delicious gravy. "The gravy hides the rest in case you're not sure what you've eaten," she joked. Virgil forced a smile to return hers. She took a deep breath. "Let's walk along the river."

Together they strolled, enjoying the sunset. He longed to reach out his hand to take hers. He felt certain he could feel her wanting to take his. When she finally spoke, she said: "I know you're very disappointed, Virgil, that we won't be married. That day in the meadow when we kissed, I..."

"You kissed me twice after that, remember," he replied sharply. "We held hands— an' I thought y' felt th' same way I did."

Another strong memory of the most memorable time they had spent together swept over Virgil, but he did not mention it. *Mebbe ya forgot. That day I caught ya a-bathin' in th' creek, in that forest meadow filled with wild flowers! I had yer clothes under m' arm, a-teasin' ya. We commenced t' gigglin' somethin' fierce! But we was afraid someone'd happen along, an' we cut it short.*

"After we came in sight of that mountain, everything changed for me," Claire said defensively. "I've decided to hire a raft on my own and float on down to Vancouver or Portland town. It will be safer than freezing to death in the mountains. You said you were thinking about going that way, overland on that road." Claire pointed to the road that led back up the bank beyond the cemetery. "So this is goodbye, Virgil."

He stopped in his tracks.

"I'm seven years older, it's just not done."

*Not done! Not done!* Her voice echoed in his ears. He turned and walked away, head down, rather than argue with the woman he loved.

When he was some distance away, he turned around and yelled, "You'll be stuck here 'til spring! I cain't swim! Goodbye, then!"

# CHAPTER 3

# The Captain's Story

CAPTAIN RUFUS AMBROSE STUBBS WAS A WELL-KNOWN CITIzen of Savannah, Georgia. His family had owned a plantation and slaves for three generations. A staunch member of aristocratic society, he was famous for throwing some of the most lavish parties in the state, and his robust size was a clear testimony to the excesses of his lifestyle.

At the outbreak of the Civil War, as he was neither a military man nor a West Point graduate, the highest rank he was offered was that of Captain of Artillery. He was promised rapid advancement to Major and then to Colonel, if he proved himself in the field. He accepted the lowly assignment, intent on making the most of it.

His first posting was downriver from Savannah, at Fort Pulaski. He was put in charge of guarding the river mouth with short-range Napoleon cannons. When the Confederacy shelled Fort Sumter, one hundred miles by sea to the north, he became an outspoken critic of Robert E. Lee's battle plan for protecting the mouth of the Savannah River from blockade.

*He insisted the walls of the fort could never be breached by enemy cannon and ordered our long-range rifle cannons moved inland. Should the fort be captured by some miracle, he said, the long-range guns could be turned on the city of Savannah, but I always knew the fight was here.*

Captain Stubbs watched helplessly as the walls of Fort Pulaski were pummeled repeatedly, and ultimately breached by long-range Yankee siege guns that were entrenched on the beaches just out of range of his Napoleons.

*We were forced to sink the Georgia, one of our Ironclads, in the Savannah River, to block the Yankee ships from sailing all the way up to Savannah! We did their work for them, blockaded ourselves in, to save the city. The General was wrong.*

27

A year later, at the siege of Vicksburg, the Confederate fort on the Mississippi River, Captain Stubbs was again put in charge of some of that fort's artillery, but this time, he insisted on access to the long-range guns. He held them out of the battle, insisting the Yankee siege guns would target them. He watched nervously while the Union forces laid rails that would bring their heavy siege guns within range of his. He was nearly relieved of duty because his superiors did not grasp the reasoning behind his strategy.

When the Union guns were locked into place, outside of what they believed was the range of the Confederate artillery, Captain Stubbs rolled his pre-calibrated long-range cannons forward and opened fire. The first shots completely destroyed several of the batteries, as well as a locomotive that was needed to pull the guns back out of range. It was sweet revenge for Artillery Captain Stubbs, but short-lived.

The fort surrendered the day after the defeat of the Confederacy at Gettysburg, and Captain Stubbs was forced to make a daring nighttime escape down-river, clutching a floating tree limb, along with many of the other officers, none of whom had any desire to be taken prisoner.

The captain tried to jam a branch of the limb into the propeller of a passing Yankee patrol boat as it steamed by in the dark. He got too close to the whirling blades, and received a painful but non-lethal leg wound.

With the Yankees now in control of the Mississippi and Captain Stubbs no longer fit for active duty, his promised rank advancement to Major was postponed. He was sent home to Savannah to recover.

A year later, Union General William Sherman burned Atlanta and began his scorched-earth march toward the sea. Savannah lay in his path.

Once his leg healed, Captain Stubbs was sure his skills at targeting artillery would again be needed. He found the defenses for the city adequate, but without the long-range siege guns that he knew could dictate the outcome.

In a surprise move, rather than fight, the local Confederate General took his ten thousand troops and left the city, leaving it undefended. Captain Stubbs immediately rallied every remaining able-bodied citizen to take up arms against the invaders.

He assured anyone who would listen, especially his nephew and only living relative, Virgil, that he had fought the Yankees twice before, and "had nearly licked them both times."

The attack never came. The mayor of the city, accompanied by a number of civic leaders that included Captain Stubbs and some of the area's prominent ladies, surrendered the city rather than see it destroyed. In the process, Captain Stubbs became a celebrity. He received more than his share of credit for saving the city from destruction.

With his head held high, he walked around Savannah as the war dragged on, a calming influence in troubled times. His very presence brought people out to shake his hand and hear any news he might have about the war.

Men saluted him, and ladies swooned at his good looks. He no longer wore his military uniform. Instead, he wore an immaculately tailored white suit. He sported a black tie, which highlighted his long blond hair, cultured mustache, and goatee. He appeared to be the perfect symbol of the past, and of a bright future.

Captain Stubbs had learned how to work a crowd. Despite the fact that his leg wound had healed, he continued to lean on his cane. He strutted around the city, his cane clicking on the cobblestones, feigning a continued need for a mobility aid.

His new command became the people of Savannah. One of the most refined gentlemen left in the city, his presence inspired confidence. People believed what he had to say, relying on his word more than on what was published in the local paper, which he eventually bought. "Even bad news can come with some hope!" he told his nephew.

He often said to Virgil, who followed along everywhere he went: "We've taken a beating, boy, but we're still standing tall!" The consistent clicks of his cane on the cobblestones reassured the citizens of Savannah, who often proclaimed: "Defeat is everywhere, unless Captain Stubbs is on patrol!"

Once Yankee troops occupied the city and paraded in the streets, the former Captain Stubbs found fewer positive things to print about the war, so he switched to preparing the city for a different kind of siege: "Hide your food. Make them Yankees live off the land. We'll still be eating ribs and black-eyed peas for dinner while they choke down their weevil-ridden hardtack!"

To maintain his reputation as a peacemaker, though, he offered a respectful salute to any Union soldiers he encountered on the streets, including special nods and smiles to their ladies.

He delivered news of the Confederate surrender at Appomattox in 1865 with his usual optimism. "We've taken a beating, but we're still here, and we still believe in the South, y'all!" His positive demeanor continued to be just what the people of Savannah needed.

Despite whatever appeared in print in the only newspaper in town, crowds still wanted to hear the news in person. The most common question was "When will the Yankee troops be gone?"

Captain Stubbs confidently stated: "Them Yankees know culture when they see it. They'll get tired of tryin' to live up to our way of life. A year from now, they'll be gone and we'll gather our grit and start over."

All traces of the life Stubbs knew began to vanish, however, as General Sherman implemented Special Order Fifteen, which confiscated and converted to federal property his remaining land along the Savannah River. Captain Stubbs was forced to change his routine. The sound of his clicking cane on his daily walks was eliminated as he became the target of affronts to his civil rights, both subtle and blatant, by the Union occupiers. They often yelled at him that he could be, "the mule on the forty acres of your previous plantation, now in the hands of former slaves."

He promoted Virgil from newspaper delivery boy to copy boy, but rather than experience a sense of fulfillment and pride at the two of them working to keep the public informed, he discovered that the war, at least for them, was just beginning.

Instead of walking about freely with his ever-present cane, his forays were by carriage, after dark. Together, he and Virgil mapped out the routes of the federal patrols, and then arranged newspaper drops in places that would avoid any contact with those soldiers. Stubbs cleverly left a single copy of his paper, held down by a stone or brick, at selected sites, giving the impression that all but one copy had been distributed before the patrols arrived.

Faced with a new challenge, that newsprint was suddenly in short supply, Stubbs changed to a weekly underground edition of his newspaper. He and Virgil distributed bundles, wrapped in burlap and hidden in cotton bales. They continued to stay one step ahead of the Yankee patrols.

The occupation troops began to watch him day and night. He was ordered to cease and desist the publication of any news not previously authorized by the current governing body, and when he refused to comply, his printing press was destroyed.

When Captain Stubbs arrived one morning at his little newspaper headquarters to find his office ransacked and the printing press in ruins, he headed for the office of the City Commander.

"This outrage is a slap in the face! I demand the satisfaction of responding as any respectable southern gentleman would. I challenge you to a duel! Name your second!" he yelled at the Union General, to the applause of the crowd that followed him to that commander's office.

Rather than granting Stubbs the battle he felt was his duty and responsibility, the former Captain of Artillery was ordered confined to his newspaper office under guard, and threatened with arrest if he attempted to continue to produce a publication of any type.

He made one last effort, in spite of the orders he swallowed like a bitter pill. Virgil delivered the last edition, which was a series of hand-written letters that Captain Stubbs smuggled to him through a crack in the office wall. In his final message to his subscribers, he exhorted: "Hold your head up, Savannah! Never walk under a Yankee flag, and feed them invaders rats instead of rabbits."

After three years of occupation by Union troops, not only had Stubbs's newspaper been destroyed, but his right to vote was revoked, and all of his country property forfeited. The loss of the remaining portion of his family's estate bothered him the most. "Without it, we're no better off than the freedmen that are living in my house or the bummers who squat on my land," he told Virgil. "You can't get ahead in this world, son, without owning property!" He thumped the boy's chest repeatedly to make his point. "None of this is right. My family has owned that plantation for three generations." *Thump, thump, thump.*

A staunch patriot, Captain Stubbs had sold the family heirlooms, horses, and furniture to support the war effort. He had quietly and unobtrusively set the last of the slaves free when the outcome of the war was no longer in doubt. None of that mattered to Sherman's troops. They knew who he was, and were determined to destroy him. Stubbs had intended to present himself to the enemy as a small landowner, interested only in growing a few peaches and tobacco on his remaining acres, with his nephew's help. Now, freedmen and lawless vagrants had taken over his plantation, and General Sherman's Reconstruction orders had stripped him bare.

Unable to find anything positive in the Reconstruction, Captain Stubbs discussed the future with Virgil. Jaw set, he proclaimed: "Time for a change of scene. The war is lost and that's bad enough, but the so-called peace is worse."

Gangs of his former comrades in arms, "bummers" as he called them, broke into his office more than once, where he was forced to remain under guard. One of the miscreants broke the captain's nose as he struggled with the man, who stormed the office intent on stealing a smoked ham. The Union guard detail looked the other way throughout the entire incident.

When his swollen nose healed, Captain Rufus Ambrose Stubbs realized that he needed to seek another way of life, and that the only permanent solution for his compulsion to be a solid citizen was to be a landowner again. He decided to go west.

---

*Virgil's Diary. Jan-yew-airy 1 1869, We borded a cargo hawler called the Santiago de Cuba, coal-burner, usin sails on a count of their aint no coal. Ship hawlin cotton bales to trade for sugar, headed for Havana. We went huggin the coast of Florida; flag of Spain blowin in the breezes. I love the open sea. Anythin is better thn bein cooped up srounded by Yankees. Captin Stubbs has met everone on board— wants there stories—if they got anything to say about the west he buys um a drink.*

*Jan 6, we travlled overland to Havana by cart, jarred my bones good! Captin Stubbs booked us passsage on a ship hawlin stuff from Europe to the Missisi Delta. He wanted us both to see New Orlians. Them Yankees spared the city like they did our Savannah.*

*Feb-yew-airy 5, We are travelin on the river by steemboat, to Saint Louee, then on to Independense, Mizouri, I think. Can't spell Missisi yet... Captin Stubbs tells all the wimmen, charmed to meet ya!!! Them laydies like im. He makes me practice speakin like them Yankees. Says we got to listen to um talk ever day.*

*Feb 13, Saint Louee is full of them thieven pickpockets, more Union troops than we can count too. I just as soon go home, missin home in Savannah.*

*Feb 15, Captin Stubbs don't like Saint Louee. Sez It don't feel right. Back on board a differnt riverboat. This one has fleas a jumpin ever-where even overbord. Captin Stubbs hardly sleeps. Up all hours talkin to someone who knows someone to find out about leadin a party west. Hes got no interest in goin back home. Got mad at me for askin.*

*Feb 20, Everwhere we walk in Independens, Captin Stubbs ackts like he owns the street, sez we shoud be proud. Not sure of what. Watch and learn he sez. He flatters them laydies. Captin is master at offerin a helpin hand too. We are learnin about the trip more ever day. He bought us riding cloths, tanned leather britches and the like,* broad brimmed hats, but mine got lifted right away. I never stold nothin, not about to start. He sez we got to have a costoom to make the right dimpression. Can't think what he means.

Feb 22, Captin Stubbs watched a pair of swindlers pickin new arivvals like us—people not thinkin about nothin cept makin there fortune out west, which they ain't got none yet. He watch um in action, re-sellin wagons and pullin stock been left untended.

March 1, Captin Stubbs offerred to hold a team and full-up wagon, with only a woman holdin them rains. She said her man follered a crowd into a saloon to hear news bout a gold strike. Captin wanted to look inside the wagon—meant no harm. The wife jumped down and dragged them kids inside the saloon, left us all alone. Woman pulled her hussbun out by the ear. First time I wondered if we was stealin that wagon. Seen one sold on the next street, for cash. We herd about it.

March 5, People in a hurry are the easiest pickin.

March 8 One fella walks with a made-up limp and broken cane from a war wound that weren't real. Told the mark he had one more newspaper to sell for to pay off a debt. His boss he said was the newspaper owner and he has the real news of the gold, the inside secksion of the paper, in his office, to keep for hisself.

The front page has a mad- up headline, Gold in Oregon! in plain site for bate. He offer to let the mark read the hole story for free, if he fetchd the inside secksion from the newspaper office round the corner. The real story is inside the weekly. Its all free, he sez. He held the horse but only for a minute. Aint nothin free in this world.

The horse spooked and bolted off. The crook too weak to foller. Paper wads from a fire cracker nearby—easy scuffed away in the street. The thief point his cane the rong way when the man comes back. Another guy grabs the horse.

March 20. Them wagon trains are leavin every day. But we aint left. When we gonna head west? I askt Uncle Stubbs and git some of that gold and free land? You recon we'll have to fight some Injuns on the way I askt Captin Stubbs? He told me he wants his own trane of wagons. He'd be wagon master. We'd keep our relasion a secred. He tuck out an ad.

*April 1 we got us fifteen Osnaburg coverd wagons to sign up, twelve riders and two Murphy wagons pulled by oxnn. We inspectd each one to make sure they had spare parts and the smaller wheels been put in front. Makes um easier to turn. We took mony up front. All there stock is outside of town were we could keep an eye.*

*April 10 We made some trips up river on our own followin the ruts from wagon tranes that alreddy went, so we no the trail.*

*April 20 We ain't gone yet.*

*April 23 We be the last trane in town now. A couple wagons left us on there own today.*

*April 25 Captin Stubbs wont say what hes waitin for.*

*April 27, Captin Stubbs is the spittin imaje of that union genral George Armstrong Custer, sponsed to be in Kansas fightin Injuns. Some one assk him why he aint no genral no more. Nobody is who they seem to be here.*

*A cavlry man who served under Custer assked Captin Stubbs about the union battle plan at the first battle of Bull Run. Custers first fight during the War. Captin dint know the locashion of the battle. It dint set well.*

*April 30 Were a leavin in the morning. Captin Stubbs been accusd of not bein that genral Custer. He dint know nuttin about that Bull Run battle.*

*April 31, We as prepared as any, made ten miles the day out.*

*May 10 Man died of a snake bite today. Nobody new what to do. Claire is helpin me with my letters and numbers. Captin Stubbs found some kind of real important Land deed. Union boys get to squat where ever they want. Maybe its worth somethin. Uncle Stubbs said, that Union man got no one to give it too, Captin kept it.*

*May 19, I think, I got it right. A homestead is one hunnert-sixty-achres. Uncle Stubbs wants enuf deeds to make up fer what he lost back home. Thinks hes still leadin them troops, charmin the Laydies, likes to give orders, makes me tend stock. Most everbody that dies is a Yankee. A spit of justis for the south as sweet as Molassess! he sez. Hes got a bunch of them Land deeds now.*

*June 10. Were a looking for a place to cross the Plat River. Wagon tipped over, lots of stuff floated a way. A horse drownd too. Uncle Stubbs is thinkin about makin another trip.*

*July 14 Greed is not a wonderful thing, Claire makes me spell it rite on paper over and over. We run out a water, lots of grumbles, saw a few graves, and stuff along the trail. Nothin I could carry.*

*July 20 We stop ever day for somethin, saw a fire way off in the distans and a dust storm, and a bunch of them runnin buffallo. We got one and it tastes good. I aint much on cookin. Claire likes to walk in the evenin but she rides all day and I walk. Her folks come down sick. She drives the wagon real good.*

*August 1 We are on flat ground agin. Some mounten way off in the distans. I think Claire likes me better then shes a sayin.*

*August 20 Both Claires parents died this week. Claire dont look good. Says she cant help me no more with my letters.*

*September 4 Two of Claires pullin stock died after eatin Arrow Grass. Shes down to 2, blames me, since I was a watchin them eat. Don't know nothin about Arrow Grass till now.*

# CHAPTER 4

# Trial by fire,
# The Reverend's Story

T HE VARYING INTERPRETATIONS OF EVENTS THAT TRANSPIRED
at the invocation service on the campus of the Methodist
School of Divinity of Chicago in 1860 would not be forgotten
by anyone who had been there, read the papers afterwards, listened
to the eyewitness accounts, or participated in one of the debates
that sprang up throughout the city as a result of those events.

Had fire from heaven descended on the campus chapel to call
out one of the least would-be ministers, local boy Donald Ricketts,
for some special service for almighty God? Did carelessness cause
an accident by a poorly-performing student, desperate to graduate,
as reported by the fire department? The school faculty members
and the community, the majority of whom were believers, saw it
one way, and the fire department, the other.

Ricketts was standing in the pulpit at the time. The number of
small fires that sprang up simultaneously in the chapel that day was
unreasonably large. He was holding a lit candelabra, which could
not have caused twelve fires to start, because the candelabra held
only six candles.

That the chapel burned to the ground, but that no one had per-
ished, and that no injuries were suffered seemed nothing less than
a miracle. The aging chapel was overdue for major restoration, or
replacement, making more than one bystander wonder if God, or
man, was hurrying things along.

A random drawing had awarded Donnie the honor of leading
the congregation of students and parents in inspirational instruc-
tion, responsive reading, and prayer. He knew the opportunity to
preach came with considerable risk, that garnering enough credit

to graduate hung in the balance, and that the faculty members grading him were going to be particularly harsh.

He had just began his portion of the service when the fire started.

Donald Ricketts was older than most of his classmates; the only student able to grow a full beard. His poor study habits had repeatedly held him back. Now, desperate to graduate, he knew he had to make a favorable impression from the pulpit that would earn him the final credits he needed to graduate. Several faculty members in attendance would be grading him. With time running out, it was "do or die" time for Donnie.

Standing tall in the pulpit, Donnie began swinging a burning candelabra over his head to make his point: "God led his people to the Promised Land by fire, a cloud of fire paving the way across the wilderness of Egypt!" He shouted the words without realizing his error. The faculty seated in the front row cringed at the inaccuracy. *The Sinai, the Sinai!* As Donnie observed their faces, he swung the candelabra overhead several more times. In the process, all six candles were unseated.

Several members of the congregation were indulging in a nap, as they had heard "Drone on Donnie" before, and knew of no reason to not stay alert during the service. Only a few individuals, including the faculty members, were awake to see the candles sail away. Within seconds, the narthex curtains caught fire. Smoke rapidly filled the sanctuary.

Donnie's eye grew wide with fear. He shouted an alarm: "Fire! Fire! Form a bucket brigade! We'll use the baptistry water!"

The ushers, who still held their offering plates, began banging on the pews to rouse the sleeping sanctuary. Most of the people in the chapel quickly left through a side door. Several students rushed for the buckets used to fill the baptistry before the service, but when only two buckets could be found, in the face of so many fires burning, Donnie ordered everyone to exit the building. Soot-faced, clutching his notes in one hand and the candelabra in the other,

Donnie was the last to exit the building. Realizing he held damning evidence, he surreptitiously pitched the candelabra back inside.

As the crowd watched the flames leap higher, and word spread that no one had been burned, someone shouted: "Surely the Lord is at work!"

"Maybe it's like the burning bush that called Moses. He didn't get burned either."

"Or a pouring out of the Holy Spirit at Pentecost, like the tongues of fire that marked each disciple."

"We should pray!"

"It's a miracle?" Donnie said tentatively, asking a question rather than adding to the groundswell.

The stunned congregation agreed that something remarkable had just happened, but what? Had "Drone on Donnie" Ricketts been called by God? "The man's beard wasn't even singed!" someone yelled.

*I'll be tossed out on my ear now for sure now,* he thought, as he wondered if anyone saw him dispose of the evidence he had so recently held in his hand—the candelabra. He didn't realize at first that the crowd was cheering him. His mouth dropped open in surprise when his classmates gathered around him, touching his robe in awe.

Catching on, he exclaimed: "I called on the Lord in my hour of need and he answered!"

The late-arriving fire department found the building engulfed in flames, the blaze impossible to extinguish. When the firemen were finally able to sift through the charred remains and piles of melted wax, the empty candelabra was discovered by what had formerly been the side exit door.

Donald's quick thinking did account for something, the faculty agreed later, as they surveyed the damage with the school trustees. They acknowledged that his actions to evacuate the chapel were probably life-saving.

Donnie discovered a small patch of wax adhered to the skin right in the middle of his forehead. Once removed, it revealed a small but visible scar, shaped like a flame. "He's been marked by the Almighty!" his classmates asserted.

As he would tell it from the pulpit for years to come, the unknown and struggling student called 'Drone on Donnie' became Reverend Donald Ricketts, man of God, transformed and inspired in an instant, by fire.

A cub newspaper reporter, eager to make a name for himself and for his copy to make the front page of the Chicago Register, listened politely to several eyewitnesses, among them student Bartholomew Titus, who had been seated in the second row of pews. He showed everyone, including the newspaperman, his Bible, which he thought he had lost in the flames. It too was undamaged. "I was in the midst of looking up a passage in the Scriptures!" he declared. "Donnie truly is a man of God! You ask anyone here. We all saw the Lord descend on him!"

The reporter's headline that was published the next day read:

### Fire-Breathing Reverend destroys Chapel!

"The question of how so many small fires could have been started from the six candles was widely discussed. Some of those who witnessed the event testified that the total was eleven, the number of Jesus' disciples, while others insisted that there were twelve separate outbreaks of flames."

The school trustees met in closed session. They discussed whether Ricketts would be awarded his degree, and one official insisted that his graduation must be linked to several conditions, including that some form of reparation would be required of him. The question of what form those reparations should take generated more questions about the entire incident.

"Not a single person was injured? How is that possible?"

"You say the man has been marked?"

"Surely, the Lord is at work in this place... or was!"

"Maybe one of those old wick lanterns sprung a leak," a long-time school alumnus turned trustee suggested. He was summarily informed that only three lanterns were lit at the time.

Donnie was summoned to the meeting. He was asked to repeat at what point he noticed there were more fires burning in the chapel than the number of coal oil lanterns, of which there were three, added to the number of burning candles, six. "I was surprised at the number of small fires," Donnie said, "and I don't have any explanation to offer."

After a few more questions, Donnie was excused. The trustees pondered the sequence of events. There seemed to be no earthly explanation why the number of fires, counting the candelabra and the lamps, totaled less than what was observed by eyewitnesses. Taken into account also were the sizable offerings received after the chapel burned.

After substantial debate, the dean of students cast the deciding vote, granting a degree to Donnie, who was delighted with the outcome. He never saw a secret document, signed by all the trustees, that explained their rationale to the faculty:

> "The best strategy is to let the debate go on in public until it plays out on its own. It's good for the ministry of the faith if one or two of the fires are believed to have been started by the Lord on high. God moves in mysterious ways, does he not? God must want the chapel replaced right now. Our newly anointed man can help rebuild it. Then, God will want him elsewhere. We need to ensure that both of these things happen."

It was my fault… I think, Donnie admitted, once the decision was announced. Or was it? As time went by, he convinced himself God had indeed intervened, making his presence known by protecting the assembly and lighting at least one additional fire, the one responsible for the burn on his forehead.

Once he was ordained as an official reverend, he was determined to help make things right with the school. "I'll help rebuild the chapel. After all, Jesus himself was a carpenter."

Several follow-up stories in the papers were veiled with cynicism:

*Fire Breathing Reverend is ordained; agrees to help*
*rebuild the chapel, then promises to leave town.*
*He'll serve the Lord with his every step, he claims.*

"I've been called forth from a burning building to preach to the unsaved savages in the west!" The reverend Ricketts declared.

When the Civil War began a few months later in April of 1861, Donald immediately enlisted. He did not drive a single nail in the new chapel, to the relief of the school faculty.

He felt at home as a chaplain in the 34th Illinois Volunteers of the Union Army. In his first letter to his parents, he wrote: "I lift up my eyes and look on the fields of new recruits for this noble cause. They are ripe for harvest."

By the time General Sherman began his march toward Savannah, Referend Ricketts had distinguished himself within the Chaplain Corps. He had worked tirelessly to provide comfort to the wounded by writing letters for the seriously injured, and by entertaining them, playing his banjo. He had made a name for himself by breaking up a number of lice gambling rings. For his efforts, he was promoted to the rank of Captain of Chaplains.

All his letters home were opened and read by his commanding officer, who discovered that the troops had revived the nickname of "Drone-on Donnie."

The diversion of betting on head lice races had been impossible to stop, during the long wait times between engagements. Despite the threat of punishment, the men hid their stables of the fastest lice in tobacco pouches or matchboxes, and took advantage of any opportunity to indulge in heavy betting on a hastily thrown-together race.

The reverend's strategy was to wait until the end of the race, and then to insist on collecting an offering from the winners, to be shared with wounded soldiers. As the men had little money, they reluctantly gave up their matches and tobacco, placing them on a pewter dinner plate, usually the same one the men used as a racetrack. "Where two or more are gathered, the Lord is in your midst and writing in the book of life faster than a winning louse!"

Once the plate was piled up with tobacco and matches, Donald would inspect the contents for lice. His superiors were impressed with his tactics.

He received several letters of commendation for his work among the troops during the remainder of the campaign in the southern states.

When the war ended in 1865, he marched proudly in the Grand Review with General Sherman's troops as they entered the District of Columbia.

After mustering out with the rest of the regiment, he returned to Chicago to look for churches to support his ministry out west. He read everything he could get his hands about the current work of other missionaries, hoping to offer his services to one of them. Despite learning of the massacre of missionary Marcus Whitman and his family, twenty years earlier, he was determined to pursue what he perceived as his true calling.

His brow furrowed with concern when he read that some of the Indians had chosen the Mormon faith. *Where are our missionaries? I should be out there. There's less and less written about the number of Indian converts and more about the need for support of the families who arrive from the east.*

He found the local congregations more interested in building schools and churches for the children of former slaves in the south "before it is too late," they told him. "Wait until the railroad goes through and reapply for support then." He heard the same message time and again. "The work out west has changed. It's about colonizing, not conversion of the Indians." He wanted to decide if that was true himself, but realized that without a sponsor, he could not afford the move.

Frustrated, he reluctantly accepted a call to go south instead of west. He worked obediently for four years in New Orleans, growing increasingly restless. He reapplied to the Methodist churches there in March of 1869 and received only a single promise of temporary support—a monthly stipend of ten dollars, for one year. He was to return at the end of a year and report his success among the Indians. He was thrilled, certain that God was finally opening doors for him.

*I wonder if relations have gotten any better between the whites and the Indians. The Cayuse Indians who killed Whitman and his wife have been dealt with. That tribe is contained on a reservation in Oregon. It's the Shoshone now who are on the rampage. That won't stop me. I'm going.*

Only one wagon train remained in Independence by the time Reverend Ricketts got there, and he was the last traveler added to the group. It was the wagon train lead by Captain Rufus Ambrose Stubbs. *He looks like General Custer.*

He purchased a horse and supplies, and left one week later, with the wagon train, bound for Oregon.

# CHAPTER 5

# Molly Mae Tucker's Story
## *March 1 1869*

B OBBY JOE TUCKER REMOVED FIFTEEN-YEAR-OLD MOLLY MAE from a Catholic boarding school in Ohio when his wife became seriously ill, and moved the family aboard the Natchez Queen riverboat, where he was first mate. He had been a deck hand and later a ship builder, well-known up and down the Mississippi River. Bullishly strong, short, and quick-tempered, his greatest weaknesses were gambling and taking offense at anyone who commented on his stature.

Bringing non-paying passengers on board and providing them with room and board required him to sign a promissory note with the captain, stipulating that Tucker would be required to work a full year at half pay in exchange for their presence. 'Bubba' did not intend to work that long.

Once settled, he charged his daughter 'Mumkin,' as he lovingly called her, with the care of his ailing wife, who was in the final stages of consumption.

Molly Mae adapted quickly to their small quarters just above the water line in the bow. Her mother spent most of her time on the narrow bed, while the girl explored every corner of the boat.

The slender young girl had no experience caring for the sick, except the few ministrations she offered a bird with a broken wing and an aging feral cat. She housed the bird in her mother's lined hatbox. The cat appeared only at meal times, and then disappeared toward the boiler room. The girl spent long hours entertaining her mother by describing the boat, each new load of passengers, the cargo, and what she saw out of the small porthole. She didn't know what else she could do to alleviate her mother's suffering.

When Mrs. Tucker died, the captain reluctantly made an unscheduled stop on a small island to bury her. Bubba and Molly Mae were the only persons who attended the funeral. Molly Mae's tears of anguish could not be quelled. "I should of done more!" she wailed.

Back on the boat, powerless to console his grieving daughter, Bubba plunged himself into his work even more, unaware that Molly Mae, who rarely saw him, was lonely. He had taken on a second shift as a relief stoker to make extra money to feed his dream of moving west. He had often talked about the trip with his wife, and had been certain that fresh air would make her well.

His dream did not perish with his wife's death. As soon as Bubba had enough money, he intended to make a better life for himself and for his daughter by heading west.

Several days before the Natchez Queen docked in Memphis to load up bales of cotton, Molly Mae got in trouble. She had kicked a passenger's son repeatedly in the shins. "He said my pigtails looked like double rat's tails!" she told her father. As the boy hopped in pain around the quarterdeck, he had continued to taunt her: "You're a river rat, river rat, river rat." Every time he spat those despised words, she had kicked him again.

Bobby Joe decided his daughter needed a companion, so when he found a small stray dog running loose, he caught it and brought it to her. She was delighted with "Tug."

Molly Mae loved life on the river, but she worried about her father's dream of going west. She observed with alarm that in trying to finance the trip, he had fallen into the habit of throwing dice with the other deckhands. He was drinking heavily as well. Her life seemed to be going steadily downhill.

*I couldn't help my mother get well. Maybe I won't be able to help father, either. I had a birthday, and…* She didn't want to complete her thoughts. Something awful had happened. Her father had quarreled with another crew member, a stoker he caught dead drunk on the job. Once Bobby Joe roused him, he had beaten the man nearly unconscious again, and then had thrown him overboard behind the stern of the boat, tethered with a length of rope. "To sober him up," he pleaded in his defense. Other members of the crew testified that the man would have surely died, had they not alerted the captain to stop the boat so they could hoist the man back on board. The Natchez Queen was damaged in the process: without maneuvering power, it drifted into a sandbar.

The captain's patience with Bobby Joe had already grown thin, as his first mate had been accused of stealing from the passengers.

After gambling away the money he had saved, Bubba had borrowed even more from the captain against his future wages, which he did not intend to stick around long enough to earn. That money was lost in games of chance as well, and as his losses mounted, the wagon and provisions he had seen in his dreams began to slip away.

One day out of Independence, he convinced the captain he was certain he had been swindled, and that he needed one last loan to catch the man in the act. The captain agreed to loan him additional funds, unaware that Bobby Joe had stolen a number of valuables from passenger staterooms, including a gold watch.

His money was lost again to the same man who had been the victor in the crap game the night before. When Bubba offered the gold watch to square the debt, the man recognized the watch as his. He pulled a small revolver as the two men stood facing each other. "You're a no-good thief!" A struggle for the gun ensued, which went off, discharging into the floor.

A cabin steward reported the incident to the captain, who acknowledged that his first mate was becoming a liability. That same day, Bubba had beaten the coal stoker and thrown him overboard.

Upon arrival in Independence, the stoker and his witnesses had gone to the local sheriff and filed a complaint. The captain lodged his own accusations against Bobby Joe of theft, assault and battery, and dereliction of duty. Bubba was promptly arrested. His trial occurred later that same day, a unanimous guilty verdict pronounced, and he was sentenced to six months of hard labor.

Molly Mae was blissfully unaware of this sudden turn of events. She knew her father had been in a fight, but she kept busy, as she did every day, running errands for the purser, chopping vegetables in the kitchen, cleaning and dusting with the maids, and playing with Tug. She did not realize he was gone until she took a sandwich to his post, and was told that he had been arrested and taken away.

Abandoned and confused, Molly Mae pieced together the events surrounding her father's arrest and conviction. No one seemed to know where he was; all she was told was that he "had to pay his debt to society by working at the county farm." She spent every waking moment of the next three days on shore, searching for information about the location of the work farm.

Her search became urgent a few days later when she heard the news that the Natchez Queen was due to leave port for Saint Louis that day. *I have to get father out or the Queen will leave us.* Her incessant inquiries had led her to a man who had recently completed his months of servitude, who directed her about a mile inland. She headed there as fast as her slender legs would take her.

Arriving at a cluster of buildings, Mollie Mae stood apprehensively in the humid morning air, fearful at being so far from "the Queen," as she called her home.

The words **"Poor FArm"** were written on a weathered cedar shingle that hung by a single rusty nail below an open hay loft above her head. To those who entered to serve a sentence for the first time, the range was from one to six months of hard labor. Repeat offenders faced punishments that were much more harsh. Shorter sentences were meted for former Union Army veterans, especially if they could get money from relatives to turn over to the proprietors. In those cases, sentences could be reduced to as few as two weeks.

Molly Mae knocked urgently on the huge sliding door that rested against the ground at the far end. The sound echoed throughout the cavernous interior of the three-story hay barn. The door shuddered at the impact and she stepped back, fearful that it might fall off the hinge and onto her. Somewhere inside a horse whinnied from its stall.

Tug rubbed nervously against her leg. She knocked again, as hard as she could. *Knock! Knock, knock!* "Is anyone there?" she called. She looked up at the open hay loft, hopeful that someone would appear. Tug gave a single bark, then lost interest, and walked to a nearby chicken pen to explore the smells.

While she waited, she recalled her father's words, which he so often repeated: "We're going west, soon as I can save up enough for the trip. We're gonna work the Columbia River, the same way the Queen works the Mississippi."

She did not understand why going west would be appealing. Aboard the Queen she had a warm and cozy life in the bow of the boat below the main deck. *Tug likes it, too.*

Bobby Joe's method of entertaining his daughter each evening had been to repeat news of the west, things heard from the passengers. His daughter realized that he thought of little else. "Not everybody's going west!" His stories squelched any sense of adventure. *Why should we leave the safety of the Mississippi?*

"Everyone should go, before they're too old, and see the rich soil, and unspoiled rivers. They say they're filled with jumping salmon."

Molly Mae overheard the stories of other passengers, too. They told of enormous bears, snakes, illness, deserts, and savage Indians. *How can he want us to live so far away from my river?*

Bobby Joe was determined that this would be his last trip down the river aboard the Natchez Queen, as he grew ever more certain that heading west was the right move for the two of them. Each bit of news was another confirmation that overruled one major risk: that they might not get there alive.

Molly Mae's thoughts were quite different: *They talk about hardships along the trail. What if things are even worse than people say?*

Her freckled, heart-shaped face was as determined as she could make it, but hid how she really felt: fearful if she failed, and even more fearful if she was successful at getting him out. *I've got to convince him to not take us out west.*

She fingered the brooch that had belonged to her mother. *It has to be worth something.* She had no idea what its value was or how much of her father's sentence could be commuted if she surrendered it. *The Queen is due to leave port. If we're not on board, we'll be left behind. What will become of us?* She sighed deeply and shook her head. *But if I can't convince him to get back on board after he's released, then what? How will I keep us on the river? We've got to be on board. Everything will be all right once we're back on the Queen. I'll work in the galley, or maybe as a cabin steward.*

Tug had moved to a rubbish pile that smoldered in the yard. "Tug!" she called, and he came eagerly to her side. She reached down to pat his head. When she straightened up, she was startled by the unwelcome presence of a huge man, towering over her. He smelled foul and looked fierce.

"Whadda ya want?" He eyed Molly Mae with an evil smile. His brow furrowed as he looked her up and down, one thing only on his mind. *Skinny as a rail. Probably won't offer much adventure.* "Come to pay a visit?" he snickered. *What's this li'l gal willin' to give up?*

There were other forms of payment that Molly Mae knew nothing about. If the wife of the prisoner couldn't come up with money, but was willing to make regular visits to the hayloft to satiate the lust of the farm's owner, the length of stay for the incarcerated could be reduced, depending on his level of satisfaction.

The unkempt proprietor and his slatternly, jowl-faced wife allowed the first family visitor to bring in inducements to prompt an earlier release only after the prisoner had been on the farm for at least a week. Their attitude was that it was just good business to get some work out of the convicts before taking money in exchange for a reduction of the term, as monies collected had to be shared with the authorities in Independence. Non-monetary inducements depended on whether the proprietor's wife was busy elsewhere.

Colvin Childs belched loudly, crudely scratched his stomach, which spilled over his belt, and spat a stream of tobacco juice, all the while ogling the adolescent. Molly Mae grimaced with disgust as residual juice dripped from his chin.

*The wife's over yonder tendin' the hogs, but I don't know... girl might be a screamer. Got a mangy yappin' dog, too.*

Molly Mae sorrowfully remembered her late mother as she held out the brooch for the dirty, smelly man to examine. *I hope my father doesn't ever have to know about this. I hope he doesn't blame me that she is dead; I did my best to tend to her. I wish I didn't have to give up this piece of my mother, especially not to such a nasty man.*

"What's this?"

"This belonged to my mother," she stammered. "Will it cover the debt, mister? My father's a good man. We just fell on hard times. He took to drink. But he's a Christian man. We've got to get back on board the Queen right away. It's due to leave port for Saint Louis today."

Childs gave a cursory glance at the brooch, and then surveyed the pigpens. "Hmmm," he grunted. *Don't see th' wife anywheres.*

Molly Mae stood waiting, trying to suppress her doubts. *Did I do enough for her? Mother's cough got worse no matter what I did. Maybe Father blames me.*

"You tradin' this fer yer daddy's time, li'l lady?" Colvin asked, looking back toward the pigpen yet again, his tongue pushing against his lower lip to move the tobacco plug around. Molly Mae nodded and followed his glance, curious what he was looking at. "Let's take a closer look. My books are inside here."

When she hesitated, Colvin responded with a gratuitous smile, revealing stubs where some of his teeth had been. She smelled garlic, sweat, and stale tobacco. "It was my mother's. She died. All our initials are on the back." She reached up to show him but he held the brooch out of her reach. *Something's not right.*

"C'mon, right inside," he beckoned. "Lessee how much time he's got left."

"All right," she reluctantly replied. She took a cautious step into the barn and stopped, waiting for her eyes to adjust to the dark. She smelled fresh hay. "We need to be on board the Queen by tonight, or we'll be left behind," she repeated.

"In a bit of a hurry, ain't 'cha?"

His rough arms encircled her shoulders, one huge, filthy hand clamped across her mouth. Tug growled. Colvin dragged the girl toward an empty horse stall deep inside the dark barn. Molly Mae thrashed wildly, trying to claw his face. He easily held her at bay, and then spun her around and caught hold of her pigtails. He was very strong, and Molly Mae froze with panic.

Tug grabbed hold of one of the man's pants legs and tossed his head from side to side, growling ferociously. Colvin threw Molly Mae into a pile of straw at the far end of the horse stall. "Don't make a sound, girlie, or I'll hay-hook th' both of you!" Tug barked and snarled. Colvin kicked him away, tripped on a loose board, and almost lost his balance. "You little mutt. Shut the fuck up! I'll teach that ankle-biter."

"Leave Tug alone!" Trapped in the narrow stall, Molly Mae searched frantically in the dark for something to keep Colvin away from her. Her hand found the long handle of a pitchfork, but Colvin had found it, too. He easily won the brief tug-of-war.

"Colviiiin!" his wife yelled from the pigpens, "we got a sow layin' on one of the piglets! An' whose yappin' dog is that?"

Colvin menacingly aimed the pitchfork at Molly Mae, and called out loudly: "Roll th' bitch over; I'm busy!"

Accustomed to seeing men fight on the deck of the riverboat, Molly Mae had learned that some fights ended quickly if one man had a weapon, like Colvin now held, whether that was a broken bottle, a gun, or a knife. *I have no weapon to fight with.* Other fights ended just as swiftly, following a kick directly between the opponent's legs, although she did not know why the man who had been kicked crumpled to the floor, howling in pain. She backed herself into the far corner of the stall, trying to gather her wits.

"No way out. You might's well give in. Betcha you'll like it and thank me." He giggled, jammed the fork into a pile of straw, and unbuckled his belt.

"An' while we're at it, tell me yer name, so I kin keep a proper record." He could see, despite the dim light, that she was eying the fork again. He knew she had no chance of reaching it. "Gonna try t' stick me with this, huh? Yer not bein' grateful!" He brought the pitchfork nearer, taunting her with it. "Go ahead, try for it."

She did. She only wanted to get close enough to kick him. Stumbling in the hay, she connected with the shin of his right leg. "Damn! You crazy li'l bitch! Yer daddy's not even here! I've a mind t' give yuh a real reamin' out." Outraged, little Tug leaped up, clamped his jaws firmly on the man's private parts, and shook his head violently. "Oh, God! Get this mutt the fuck offa me! I tole you th' truth! He ain't here, left early this mornin'!"

Molly Mae was stunned. "I don't believe you!" she screamed.

"Colvin! You git yer lazy ass over here an' help me roll this sow!" his wife shrieked.

Molly Mae ducked around Colvin, ran out of the barn and headed straight for the pigpen. Through a fit of coughing caused by the overwhelming stench, she announced to Colvin's wife Marabel, who was bent over an enormous sow: "I come to get my father out."

"Who th' hell're you? Know anything 'bout pigs? Wade on in. Help me free little squealy there, 'n then I'll see what I c'n do. Ate so much she cain't move, I reckon." Marabel was knee-deep in the mud of the foul-smelling pen.

"My name is Molly Mae Tucker."

"Good. Now get yer bottom in here an' give a hand." She turned back to her work, revealing the backside of bib overalls, covered in manure. A squealing, squirming piglet, one of twelve, thrashed wildly to get free from under the belly of an enormous sow.

Molly Mae was well accustomed to the oil and grease of the Queen's equipment, but the thought of stepping into manure in her copper-toed boots, and wrestling a muddy sow in her flowered calico dress made her shudder. *If I want to get my father out of here, I've got to use my wits.*

She stepped cautiously into the pen and confronted the woman: "I came to get my father out! The man in the barn was going to take something of mine to pay off Father's fine, and then he said my father's not here!"

"First things first, Molly Mae." She motioned for the girl to put her hands close to hers. Together, they tried, without success, to roll the sow over.

"Tucker, huh? Put s'more elbow grease to it an' let's try again. I'll tell ya when. Ready? Now! Push! Again!" The women strained mightily, but succeeded in rolling the huge sow only a few inches, not enough to free the piglet.

Taking a breather, Marabel looked at her helper more closely. "M' full name's Marabel Lee, but th' prisoners here just call me Marabel Lee," she said ingratiatingly, with a garlic-breath smile. She wiped her face with the back of her hand. "Tucker? Whadda ya know about pigs? An' where's my mister?"

"Still in the barn, with Tug. He's my dog. The man took him." Molly Mae replied.

"Oh, my Colvin don't like dogs," she said.

"He said if I would come help you roll the sow, he'd give me my dog back and help me find my father," Molly Mae lied, fingers crossed behind her back.

"What's yer dog's name again, sweetie?" Marabel asked.

"Tug, like the big round boat. Tug's pretty fat, 'cause he eats from every table on the Queen. That's my home too, the Queen."

"Gotcha. Go fetch the pig's feed bucket, over yonder. Sow shouldn't have no more, she's et ever'thing already, stuffed herself with alla th' milk I put out fer th' little ones. Sow's tits went dry too early. Been a pain in my backside fer nigh on a week now, drinkin' up th' milk money," Marabel groused. She saw the potential for free labor from Molly Mae, and wondered how she could trick the girl into staying at the farm.

"Let's not give any more to the sow," Molly Mae suggested. "Let's put the food in this next little pen where the piglets can get to it. The sow is too big to fit through the slats, but she'll be all right if she can see them eating."

"Worth a try, I guess."

Eleven hungry piglets streaked for the feed, spread in the adjacent, much smaller pen, within eyesight of the sow, who snorted loudly and stood up. The trapped piglet wiggled free, eager to get a long overdue meal. Marabel caught it by the front legs as it raced by, giving it a brief inspection before letting it go. "Don't look hurt none to me."

"What about my father?" Molly asked urgently.

"Tucker, yeah, mate on th' Natchez Queen. He ain't here. Like the mister told you. Riverboat captain come an' paid th' fine this mornin'. Took'm away hour 'r so ago. Said he couldn't steam down river without him. Left in a big hurry. Long gone now. I gotta say, though, yer daddy made friends here real fast, once he sobered up. Said his daughter'd be comin' to visit, didn't say when. He yer only kin?"

Molly Mae nodded dumbly.

Marabel continued: "Said he lost his wife, but I heard that one b'fore. You lose your mama, honey?" She didn't wait for a reply. "Ever'body's got a hard-luck story. Yer daddy left a note inside an envelope, with a coupla names on it. Don't make no sense t' me. Got it right here, in m' pocket. Ain't got no money in it, I already checked."

She handed a folded-up note to Molly Mae, and at that moment, a long single blast from the Natchez Queen's whistle drifted toward them. *"TOOOOT!"* Molly Mae knew that sound well. The boat was leaving the dock. Billows of black smoke were visible off in the distance. *She'll get up steam and head out in the channel under power in the next ten minutes.* "No!" she moaned.

Marabel grabbed her arm. "Yer too late, honey. Stay here with me. Mebbe you c'n catch it on th' way back up river next month."

Molly Mae wanted to run for the docks, but felt as if her legs had turned to stone as panic and shock threatened her senses.

"I got room in th' back of th' house," Marabel continued. "Food's not much but we got plenty. You'll hafta earn your keep, but yer prob'ly used to that."

"Thank you, no! I have to catch the Queen. My daddy thinks I'm on board." With the note in hand she willed herself to run, calling out for Tug as she sped away.

Colvin bellowed from the barn: "Hold onta that bitch! I ain't finished with her! I'm agonna kill her!"

"Whadda ya mean, Colvin, yer gonna butcher ol' Prudence here 'fore she's done raisin' these piggies? At least wait 'til she comes in heat again! We c'n git at least another dozen outta her!" Marabel yelled in reply.

"No, dammit! Hold onta that Tucker bitch! I'm gonna kill her mutt, an' then I'm gonna drown her!"

Mollie Mae didn't stop running until she reached the docks. The Natchez Queen was just rounding a far bend in the river, nearly out of sight. *Impossible to catch it now.* Out of breath, she began to sob. *How could this happen?* She stood on the rough wooden planks of the busy dock, as workers hauling huge bales of cotton maneuvered around her.

She unfolded the piece of paper inside the envelope. *How could he leave me? He needs me to take care of him now, with Mama gone.* She sat on a pile of rope, wiped away the tears, and read the note she tried to hold steady with shaking hands:

*"Willard Clark, trustworthy, headed to Oregon. With Stubbs party. Look for wagon master who looks like General Custer from the war. Departs April 30, Independence, Missouri. Needs Nanny for his missus and little one. Get to Oregon, Molly Mae. Love, Papa."*

She looked down river again and began running as fast as she could until she reached the end of the dock. "Father!"

She strained her neck, looking around barrels and bales, in hopes the Queen was on its way back. *Why doesn't Father turn the boat around? He must know by now that Tug and I are not on board.*

A minute later, only narrow strings of black smoke from the stacks were visible as they drifted like snakes over the water. *The Queen left us, Father left us.* Tug let out a small bark. "You got left too, boy," she said. She lifted Tug up to her lap and held him tightly until he squirmed and whined to be let down.

*I just need to wait right here. It won't be long and the Queen will round that bend in the river,* she told herself.

She improved her appearance, smoothing her hair and straightening her bedraggled dress. The wrinkles disappeared, but her memory of the struggle at the farm did not. *They know I don't have any kin. What if they come looking for me, and make me a prisoner at the Poor Farm?*

When the sun had set and The Natchez Queen had not returned, she stood up and straightened her dress again, while she continued to look downstream. *He's gone. Maybe he blames me for Mother's death.* A gusty warm breeze sprang up. She turned and faced it squarely, letting it blow her hair. She released her pigtails and ruffled her hair, the way she always did aboard the Queen, when she was standing on the quarterdeck watching the world go by.

Another riverboat arrived and was unloading passengers. Natchez III was written in large letters, painted on the side of the pilot house.

*I wonder if all the boats are the same inside? Maybe there's room in the crew quarters of the Natchez III. Maybe I can work for my keep in the galley.*

The Natchez III had the same comforting smells she knew well. Even from the end of the dock, the smell of fresh-baked flour biscuits and pan-fried chicken reached her, making her empty stomach churn. *Mid boat—main deck.* Soot and steam from the overhead stacks venting the two wood-fired boilers filled the air around her. They blended with the heavy smells of grease and lubricating oil. *Boiler deck—below the galley.* From the main deck closest to the loading ramp came the sharp smell of polished leather from the tack of horse-drawn carriages, lined up and ready, near burlap-wrapped cotton bales. The passengers would be unloaded first, accompanied by scents of facial dusting powder, shaving cream, and cologne.

The warning bell on the Natchez III sounded an alarm. *Clang! Clang! Clang!* The stern mooring line had slipped off the bollard. Only a single bowline held the boat to the dock. Strained to the breaking point, stretched tight by the strong current, the Natchez III swung wildly and banged against the dock.

Four men, two on the boat and two on shore, were shouting at each other over who was at fault. The men on the boat struggled to pull the heavy line back in. The men on shore were trying to throw a much smaller rope to the boat to attach to the larger mooring line.

Passengers trying to disembark down the steep gangplank were tossed about as the boat swung away from the dock. A young woman lost her balance and pitched over the side into the rushing water, as several other persons fell onto the quay and dock. "Help!" the woman cried.

*There must be something I can do,* Molly Mae thought.

The woman in the water was not a strong swimmer and would sweep past Molly Mae in seconds. Molly Mae dropped down on her stomach on the dock and stretched out her hands. "Hey! Over here!" Their fingers touched and after a brief struggle their arms were firmly clasped together. With Molly's help, the woman grabbed onto one of the dock pilings. She gasped: "I didn't expect to take a swim today." The girl's parents quickly appeared and hoisted their daughter back up onto the dock. The trio hurried back toward the gangplank to find a blanket and to retrieve their belongings.

Molly Mae dried her hands, and then sat on the dock with her feet dangling over the side. She re-read the name her father had scribbled on the scrap of paper. When she looked up, the young woman was standing next to her, her long single braid of hair still dripping wet, a blanket wrapped around her shoulders. "I wanted to thank you; I didn't want you to think I was ungrateful. My name is Claire O'Connor. I'm from County Cork."

"Is that up-river?" Molly Mae asked.

"No, we're from Ireland," Claire said with a smile. "We came here to buy a wagon and supplies. Those are my parents over there, Anna and Sean. We're going to Oregon, to try farming again. Is this your little dog?"

"His name is Tug, like the boat. He's fat 'cause he eats from all the tables on the Natchez Queen. That's my home. At least, it was. You can pet Tug, if you want. See how he wags his tail? I think he likes you already."

"We're going all the way in a wagon with a canvas top to keep out the rain," Claire said excitedly, patting Tug's head. "I plan to draw pictures of the prairie, the animals and everything! I've already drawn one of the Natchez III. Would you like me to draw one of Tug? Are you going to Oregon, too?" Claire didn't wait for an answer to either question. "I'm supposed to ask around to find the wagon camp."

"On my paper here, it says there's one called Stubbs Party. He looks like General Custer, from the war. It says they're leaving in a few days." She handed the paper to Claire to read for herself.

"What war would that be, lassie?" Claire's father asked.

Molly Mae looked into a large round red face with a broad smile. "Mr. Lincoln's war. It's over now."

Claire handed the note back.

"Do you know where the wagon camp is, then?" Claire's father asked.

From somewhere upriver came a shrill whistle. Another steamboat was announcing it was arriving and would need a place at the dock. *Soon I'll hear the bell*, Molly Mae thought. *It tells the stokers to stop throwing wood into the boiler.*

Molly Mae shook her head. She watched the boat work its way toward the dock, imagining it was her boat, The Natchez Queen. *I wish father was on deck, waving to me.*

Claire and her parents made their way toward the town, following a crowd of others.

There seemed no one choice better than the other: *I could stay and hope Father comes for me, or leave and find Mister Clark.* She began to run toward Independence. Tug was barely able to keep up.

She caught up with the O'Connors. Running up next to Claire, she greeted the beautiful young lady: "Hello, again! I have decided that I'm going to Oregon, too. I'm going to be a nanny for Missus Willard Clark along the way, like it says in my note. She's due any day, and they already have a young'un. I like pictures. May I see the one of the Natchez III?"

*I will be all right. I will be a good nanny for the little ones, and I won't complain. Won't be afraid. Father will come for me out in Oregon. He will be proud of me. He will take us back to my river and back to my Queen.*

## CHAPTER 6

# Claire O'Connor's Story, Ireland 1849

C LAIRE O'CONNOR WAS DREAMING.

*I am five years old. The wind is blowing in my face. I am filling my little bucket from the wooden trough. I look up to see if I have bothered the tall animal that keeps the water trough full. It moves and never speaks, but I'm sure it's alive. The head moves in every direction on windy days, looking for something. It has a tail, too; it's flat, but never wiggles.*

*What kind of animal are you?*

*It doesn't look like the other animals in my big book of circus animals. It has a large head and a small tail, so I know it's alive. It stands on four long legs, like a giraffe. It never runs away. "What shall I call you? You're not a giraffe. What is your name? Giraffe just won't do."*

*I must take the bucket to the house. This is my chore today. I lift it up with both hands and down to the ground. I know there are thirty steps to the kitchen door—I begin counting. "One...two...three..."*

*I stop and look up. "What is your name? I am Claire Louise O'Connor."*

*It has a skinny trunk, like the elephant in my book, but much longer. That must be how it sucks the water up. "What shall I call you? Elephant just won't do. What is your name? Are you both a giraffe and elephant?"*

*When the head moves 'round and 'round, I see long arms move, like an octopus has. They move up and down. "What shall I call you? Octopus just won't do. Are you part giraffe, part elephant and part octopus? Why don't you speak?"*

*"I will give you a special name. Hmmm. You have a large head and tail, legs like a giraffe, a truck like an elephant, arms like an*

61

*octopus, and you like water. I will borrow letters from each animal: 'O' and 'C' from octopus, 'G I R' from giraffe, and 'E L' from elephant. Your name is 'Ocgirel!'"*

*"Hello, Ocgirel! Thank you for my bucket of water! Can I draw your picture?"*

*Creak...creak, hee. Creak...creak, hee.*

*Ocgirel is speaking to me! "You have a very loud voice! You sound angry!"*

*"Creak, creak yee...squawk. Creak yee, creak yee... Squawk, bang! Bang! Bang! Bang! Bang!*

*"I've never heard such a loud voice. Don't you have a quiet voice?"*

*I walk faster, headed toward the house...four, five six. When I get to ten, my fingers hurt. The bucket is heavy. "Ouch!"*

*I am brave at first, then I am afraid. I walk faster. Eleven, twelve, thirteen...*

*"This is my water! Mine! Mine!"*

*I put the bucket down, and push it from behind, using my legs. The bucket is stuck! How many steps are left to reach the house? Seventeen. I wrap my arms around the bucket and hold on tightly. "You can't have it back!"*

*I cross my arms. I am angry. "I gave you a special name!"*

*I kick the bucket over and run for the house. "If I can't have it, you can't either! I don't feel so brave!"*

*I close the door and peek out through a window. I call for help. "Mother! Father!" No one answers. Did they leave me all alone?*

*My broomstick horse stands in the corner of the kitchen. I could ride away, but then who would protect the house from Ocgirel?*

*I mount my horse and feel brave. "Easy, boy." He is scared, too. I find my father's felt hat with the feather and put it on my head. The long iron fire-poker mother uses in the kitchen will be my lance. I'll charge and make Ocgirel behave!*

*From outside there is a loud sound. Crash!*

*I slowly open the kitchen door and peek out. Ocgirel lays on the ground. My empty bucket is right where I left it. It looks like Ocgirel has lost all his teeth; they lay scattered along the path. The tail no longer wiggles in the wind. The long legs and trunk are bent and broken. I ride slowly up to Ocgirel and poke it several times.*

*"I am sorry that I took the water, Ocgirel."*

*Papa comes out from the barn. He puts oil in its mouth, then he tips Ocgirel back up on its legs. The head and tail move in the wind, just like before, the long arms move up and down and water fills the trough again. My papa is very smart. He has brought Ocgirel back to life! He is the bravest man in the world.*

*"Was it hungry? Can we take it to America?"*

*Then I wake up.*

# April 30 1869
## Independence, Missouri [twenty years later]

THERE WAS AN ABSENCE OF FAMILIAR SOUNDS OUTSIDE THE WAGON when Claire awoke, but many new ones. Her long single braid of ebony hair had come undone in the night and she quickly rewove and tied it, fumbling in the dim morning light with the flimsy cloth tie. Straining to catch a glimpse of herself in the little tin mirror, her smooth complexion showed only faint lines of pressure from a heavy sleep against a pillow filled with straw. Her green eyes sparkled with excitement as she tried to identify all the news sounds and smells that drifted inside the canvas cover. *I don't hear the usual crackling fire, the rattling of dishes – but the smell of damp wood smoke is in the air.*

*I didn't hear the crow of the banty rooster before daybreak, either.* That colorful, aggressive, undersized bird had appeared out of nowhere, and strutted around camp preening before a harem of hens, all of which were much larger. His loud, incessant crows before daybreak prompted choruses of angry shouts and several fruitless attempts to drive him off, wring his neck, or put him in a stew pot. *I wonder if someone finally caught him.*

She heard the whinny of nervous horses, and the ground seemed to shake as oxen stomped. She sat up, listening more closely. Someone hurried by, leading a horse; she heard rapid footsteps and the rhythmic patter of horse's hooves. The wagon tongue jolted, startling her. Her heart beat wildly. *We're leaving for Oregon today! Who knows what's out there? We're leaving for Oregon on my birthday!*

*Papa must have already doused the fire and lit his pipe. I don't want to miss anything! Why didn't someone wake me so I could help prepare breakfast?*

She grabbed her clothes, intending to dress quickly, but stopped abruptly when a package tumbled from beneath her pillow onto the wooden floor of the wagon. *What was that?* She searched until she found it, and knew immediately what it was: *my birthday present! They didn't forget, after all!* She hugged the package briefly to her chest, and twirled in a circle in the narrow space next to the bed. The wagon lunged forward with a jerk, she lost her balance, and landed back on the bed.

The package was wrapped in colorful cloth, tied loosely with a slender thong of leather. Claire swung her long braid of hair over her shoulder and wiped the sleep from her eyes. She slowly untied the leather bow, savoring the moment, yet eager to get outside. The thrill of expectation over the contents of the package, and of the preparations for the imminent departure of the wagon train, made her giggle with excitement.

Unwrapped, the package revealed a sunbonnet and the sketch book she had asked for several weeks before. She donned the bonnet, delighted with the green, white and orange colors, and tied the strings firmly under her chin. *The colors of the Irish flag, absolutely perfect!* She eyed herself in the mirror, and realized that the wagon had surged forward and was rocking from side to side. She struggled to finish dressing in a hurry, but the forward movement of the wagon, coupled with her unusual anxiety to get outside, made the simple task of tying her shoes difficult. When she finally finished, she flung the wagon flap open, and breathed deeply, relishing the cool morning air.

Molly Mae waved half-heartedly, tears staining her face. Sadness flowed over Claire; she knew the trek to Oregon would be difficult for her new friend without little Tug. *He just vanished. I know she's looked everywhere.*

Behind Claire's wagon, the camp emptied quickly. No longer in the familiar circle, wagons and riders were forming up side by side. Captain Rufus Stubbs rode by, waving his hat. "Move out!" he shouted. "Free land for everyone out west!" Thundering whoops of approval from occupants of the thirty-five wagons rang through the air.

Claire stepped down from the back of the wagon, and nearly tumbled to the ground. *I forgot, we're moving.*

Her father was walking next to the oxen. He removed his pipe from his mouth, and waved to her, smiling broadly.

"Where's mother?" Claire called.

"She's leading the team! Happy birthday!"

Claire ran to him, and gave him a hug. "Oregon, here we come!" she exclaimed. "Thank you, thank you for the sketch book! What shall I draw first?"

"How about our home on wheels and your two favorite oxen?" he suggested. "Bess and Tillie are in the lead today."

At mid-day, the wagons stopped to rest the stock. As Claire sat, sketching, she thought: *What will there be for us out west? I want so much for Papa to be successful this time. I know he's disappointed about our failed farms in Indiana and Iowa. I wasn't strong enough to swing the scythe; I wasn't much help. He tried to do everything by himself. How many years it is now we've been in America? Nineteen? Twenty? He has tried so hard; he's tried everything.*

*Tonight, Papa and Mama will sleep under the wagon again, giving me the bed inside. I should be out from under their wings by now. I should have a man of my own. Why don't I? I turned twenty-five today.*

*My new diary. April 30th 1869. Happy birthday to me! I received a new bonnet, to wear in the sun, and a sketchbook. I've decided to use it for a diary, too. We left for Oregon today. Clouds but no rain. Papa is certain we will be successful this time. He has heard that everything grows in Oregon. We made eighteen miles in our new wagon. We have four oxen. I've named two, because they are my favorites, Bess and Tillie. A boy named Virgil helped Papa care for the stock today.*

*May 3 There isn't a single unmarried man my age in the train. Captain Stubbs, the leader of our party, has kept us going west. He has said a hundred times already, "Keep the sun at your back in the morning, and in your eyes in the afternoon." Molly Mae no longer has nanny duties. The baby died. She cried and cried along with the Clarks. We buried it along the trail. I put one of my hair ribbons on its tiny grave. I wish there was someone to talk to.*

*May 10 Virgil seems nice, but he's full of himself. He wants to pose for me to sketch a picture of him. He loves grits. He already lost his hat, and he brags that he's going to walk barefoot all the way to Oregon. We'll see how long that lasts.*

# PART II

October 11 1869
The Dalles, Oregon

# CHAPTER 7

# The Night Journey

**B**Y FIRELIGHT, DECISIONS WERE CHANGED, THEN CHANGED again on what to do: whether to wait for a raft that might not come until spring, or to risk attempting to traverse the mountain pass.

Virgil built a small campfire by sparking flint against the steel blade of his knife. He sat, gazing into the flames, wondering what his uncle planned to do.

*He said onct he owns land somewheres, he kin live by 'is own rules again.*

*He asked me t' ride along that first night outta Savannah, so that th' stolen horse c'd be returned 'fore daylight. Them Yankees done took ever'thing from him. I thought he intended t' keep th' horse, but he said it had to be returned, a question of honor, he said.*

*We rode double along th' river, dodgin' Yankee patrols, all th' way to th' coast. He warn't about to face no Yankee general again.*

*He had me on 'is mind when he stopped to rest th' horse. He said what would I do iffen I was stopped by a Union patrol on th' way back to th' city. He said he knowed that if I was caught with a stolen horse, I'd be punished good 'n hard, 'n they'd prob'ly have a necktie party 'n hang me then 'n there.*

*I reckon 'twas right then I decided I warn't gonna go back neither, but I purely wasn't ready to tell him that. We got goin', stoppin' again close by where th' ironclad CSS Georgia were sunken. We got down offen th' horses 'cause he took a notion t' takin' a long last look at her layin' there.*

*"This th' spot, Cap'n Stubbs?" I asked him.*

*"Yes, son."*

*I allus called him Capt'n after that.*

*"They sunk her there," he said, pointing out across the river. "We had to keep her out of the hands of the Yankees that took the fort in sixty-two. We have one more stop at Fort Pulaski. There, we'll say our good-byes."*

*Th' tide was out, so we rode along the riverbank. We ended up straight across from th' island fort.*

*"Remember this place," he insisted. "It should never have fallen. But just like what happened at Vicksburg, the generals couldn't see what we had."*

*He snuffled a bit. He wiped his nose with a fancy hankie he kept in a waist pocket.*

*I asked: "They took yer big guns away, back upriver, right, Cap'n? What ya would've used to guard th' city?"*

*He nodded.*

*Th' mornin' sun was comin' up. We c'd see th' outline of th' fort, just like a framed pitcher. Cap'n pointed at th' north wall. "They turned it into a prison. If I'da had the Brooke rifles back then and mounted them there, they'd have never taken the fort." I c'd just almost taste th' bitterness in his mouth, while he talked: "General Lee said the fort could never be taken by bombardment, but I knew different. The Brooke had a range of five miles and shot a projectile weighing sixty-four pounds. We had everything else we needed: position, food, and ammunition. The Union boys mounted ten-inch guns on the beach over there." He pointed offen into th' dark, an' I knew he was as good as livin' those days again.*

*"They were just out of our range. They pounded the walls 'til they give way. We had no choice but to surrender then. We had only forty-seven short-range cannons to defend the fort, but we could have mounted more than hundred." He looked down at th' ground an' shook 'is head. "I tried to tell the general, the fight is here, not in Savannah! Maybe if I'd gone to military college he would have listened.*

*Someday, it will be different." He put those hands of his on m' shoulders. "I'm going out west where I can own land again. You really should leave me here and ride on back now. If you take care to return the horse before a patrol sees you, you'll be all right."*

*"I got nothin' left in Savannah, Cap'n Stubbs."*

*"Well, then, let's find a ship with room for two passengers. We'll let the Yankees find this horse on their own."*

An hour passed. Virgil's fire was burning low. He had no more wood, so he blew gently at the base of the smoke until a small yellow flame sprang up again.

*First day outta Independence, was when I met Claire. She looked so purdy. Looked a danged sight more healthy'n she does now. She smiled at me, an' we just commenced to talkin' non-stop. She showed me a few pitchers she drew herself. I think mebbe that's when I fell fer her, right then.*

Captain Stubbs called out from the darkness, disturbing Virgil's reverie. "Holster boy!?" Virgil stood up as his uncle appeared, leading his horse.

"Why'd ya call me that, Cap'n Stubbs?"

"You give up your holster over Claire?" he asked, throwing Virgil's holster for him to catch. He didn't wait for an answer. He handed Virgil an official-looking document with the words **Land Deed** written across the top. Virgil knelt close to the fire and studied it, pointing at the words he didn't recognize, trying to sound them out. When he finished reading, he said stubbornly: "I don't want no deed fer land in Wyoming that belongs to no dead man."

"Don't y'all be so sure, Virgil. Mister and Missus Palmer can still play a part in the lives of us, the living. Just like an old dead sticker brier that still stands, it protects the new growth. Makes a dandy trellis for it to climb on. You and I are that new growth."

Virgil was unconvinced, but Stubbs wasn't finished.

"When General Pemberton heard Lee was beat at Gettysburg, he gave up Vicksburg the next day. The south was cut in two. Let's don't do the same."

Virgil looked puzzled.

Stubbs smiled at him: "One battle lost doesn't mean the next one will be."

The two fell silent, prisoners to their thoughts, until Stubbs said in a soft voice, "I seem to always make my escape in the dark."

Virgil asked, "Are we leavin' now?"

"I heard in town, our friendly northerners have formed an assembly. They're planning some kind of action, and they might not wait 'til morning. Too many people have died along the trail, they claim. They have to blame somebody, so that's me. Us. They plan to make me lead half of the party over the road and come back and help the others later, those that agree to winter here. If I won't..."

"What, Cap'n?"

"Then they'll try to string me up," he said calmly. "They say I've given them no acceptable route to the valley. As if that was in my hands. They say I haven't fulfilled my contract. Well, I'm not giving them their money back after we come this far." Stubbs removed a forty-five Schofield revolver from his waistband, and handed it to Virgil, butt first. "My Schofield kept me safe. Now it will keep you safe. Be careful. It's loaded."

Virgil jumped to his feet. "We gonna fight them Yankees, Cap'n?!"

"No, we're not a-gonna fight. I'm leaving tonight. They already guessed you're my kin, so if they take me, they have to get you, too."

The gun in Virgil's hand trembled. "We're beat here, ain't we?"

His uncle didn't answer the question. He stated: "We have to split up for a while. You take that Schofield and the land deed and head east to Wyoming. I'm going north to Montana. Change your name to Palmer, like on the land deed there. Homestead them acres for a year, and then we'll meet up in the spring. Be at Fort Laramie no later than the first of June. The miners I met in town say there's gold near the Clearwater, and all the way across to the Black Hills. If there's any truth to it, a man can still get rich out here. There's nothing waiting for us in that valley we've been headed for except a hangman's rope."

"'Cept Claire," Virgil countered.

Captain Stubbs seemed not to hear. "I'd planned to bring one more party across the plains, but I hear the railroad's through to the coast. I'd hoped to collect a few more land deeds off any Yankees that pass on. That's how I come by the one you're holding. I didn't rob the Palmers of anything else. In my book, I just took back what should've been given back to me after the war. I'm getting my land back a piece at a time."

"I comed this far t' be with Claire, Cap'n."

"I know. I saw the initials you carved on the holster there. Never was a big secret. You put that gun in the holster before you drop it. We both have different business to attend to now."

"I just hafta see her again, an' try to explain better."

"You do, you're taking a risk. She'll see the gun."

"I don't," Virgil fired back, "I'll never know if she might change 'er mind someday iffen I stay."

72

"Suit yourself." He retrieved his horse from a nearby bush and returned to Virgil's dying fire. "Verin Palmer was kin to Union General William Jackson Palmer of Pennsylvania. Palmer used to brag about it. That's what you tell everybody back in Wyoming, or in the valley, if you go on over the mountain. Palmer is your new name now. Use it to cover your tracks. Hang the deed on the wall of your cabin for everybody to see. Don't get hung, waiting too long to make up your mind whether you're going east or west!"

"She won't go back east. Told me as much."

Stubbs mounted his horse, and said thoughtfully: "You could lose either way. If you follow her to the valley and she says yes or no, or if you get caught along the way.

"I was beat at Vicksburg, too. I thought we had a chance there, but sometimes things are taken out of your hands and you don't have a choice. Here, we both do. I could sell the other land deeds, rather than pick through them for the best. Either way, I win. I stay here, I die. You'll have to live with your decision. I always thought a man built his future with his hands, his head, and his heart. Maybe out here it's different. Maybe out here you have to bend the odds any way you can." He extended his hand to shake Virgil's. "Keep an eye on your backtrail whichever way you go."

Virgil slowly took his hand, his eyes filling with tears. *Am I ever never gonna see you no more?*

"Eat more molasses, holster boy," Stubbs said with a smile. He turned his horse to leave, then stopped, dismounted and gave Virgil a long hug.

For a moment, neither could speak.

"Don't drink the water, and boil your coffee," Stubbs said, sniffing, tears in his eyes. "It keeps the drizzly shits away." He mounted again and rode off.

Virgil Stubbs never saw his uncle again.

# CHAPTER 8

# "And That's What's the Matter"

O<small>N OCTOBER THIRTEENTH THE SKY WAS UNUSUALLY CLEAR,</small> but the weather was bitterly cold and windy. Reverend Donald Ricketts needed inspiration. The Wascopam Mission, a local church run by the Methodists, had invited him to lead a revival, but not the kind he had in mind.

As with the other churches he had visited, he discovered that the Methodists no longer provided aid to the local tribes; their only interest was in the immigrants who arrived, weary, sick, and exhausted, but sometimes with a little cash. *I hoped for something different from my people. How can I persuade them to return to the original mission of Jason Lee?*

Since arriving in The Dalles he had called at every church he saw, regardless of denomination, and had proposed a joint revival that would "renew, reunite and reignite." He intended to lead the faithful back to their original mission work to the Indians. He did not mention to the Protestant representatives that he was also calling on the Catholics, or vice versa.

Any excitement the word 'revival' brought faded when he expounded on the details of what he had in mind. Not understanding why he was meeting with such resistance, he pushed on from one church to the next, saving the Methodists for last. He felt certain he could persuade them.

"We are already changing the lives of the unfortunate children of former slaves in the east," he told the Methodists. "I have assisted in that effort for the last eight years, Brothers and Sisters. Bringing Christianity to the Indians again is why I have been sent here. The Cayuse and Nez Perce were whom the great Reverend Jason Lee was first called to serve, right here at Pulpit Rock, as were the Whitmans, and we must call for them to be brought into the fold again!"

The congregation reluctantly agreed to hear more; however, during the first planning session, his call for a meeting with the local church leaders was met with stony silence, instead of the reaction he expected of his enthusiastic words being punctuated by calls of "Amen," and "Preach it, Brother!"

What he did hear was a man who shouted: "Beggars, thieves, killers! Ask Marcus and Narcissa Whitman! See what it got them!"

"But they were on the other side of the river, and that was more than twenty years ago," he argued.

The naysayer stood his ground. "You're *new* here, Reverend. We got troubles of our own. You're preachin' in the wrong place, to the wrong crowd. Follow the river east to the Clearwater. And good luck convincing the miners there to give anything to the Nez Perce."

Heads nodded in agreement.

Reverend Ricketts was forced to acknowledge that this church, like all the others, was barely holding on financially. The stable and permanent population of The Dalles was shrinking. A new gold strike on the Clearwater River in northern Idaho was shifting families, miners, and speculators east, just as the man had said.

In addition, he learned that the first floating salmon cannery on the Columbia River was due to open, but not on this side of the river, which meant the exodus of yet another segment of the population of the already small town.

Ricketts rode along the ridge above the town, looking for a spot that would allow him to see the entire area clearly. He reined in his horse Scout at the cemetery where only a few days before he had led the service for the Palmers.

He dismounted, walked past the gate that had been tossed aside, and began reading the names on the headstones and crosses. When he arrived at the Palmer's graves, he thought about offering a short prayer, but didn't. His feelings about them were suddenly in conflict with his mission to the Indians. *They say you shot yourself rather than go on without your wife. That's not very Christian, Mister Verin Palmer. God is the authority, not man.*

Feeling guilty for being judgmental, he looked skyward and queried: "Why am I here in Oregon, Lord?" *There is no mission here, like I expected there would be. Nothing says things are any different over there across the river or in the valley. I don't know where I am supposed to go.* The scar on his forehead throbbed and burned, as it usually did when he was frustrated or upset.

For the first time during his long journey west, he unwrapped the banjo that hung from his saddle, hidden for six months in the rifle scabbard. It was one of his few prized possessions. He sat on a headstone, plucking each string, tightening the corresponding tuning peg. *I played almost every day for the wounded Union boys in the field hospitals.*

*There were several songs the boys requested over and over: Stephen Foster's 'Beautiful Dreamer' was one. It became a favorite of mine, too.* He began to play and sing:

> "Beautiful dreamer, wake unto me,
>  Starlight and dewdrops are waiting for thee.
>  Sounds of the rude world, heard in the day,
>  Lull'd by the moonlight have all passed away!
>  Beautiful dreamer, queen of my song,
>  List' while I woo thee with soft melody.
>  Gone are the cares of life's busy throng.
>  "Beautiful dreamer, awake unto me!
>  Beautiful dreamer, awake unto me!"

He followed that song with another of Stephen Foster's tunes, *'We are coming, Father Abraham.'* He changed the word "bayonets" to "wagons."

> "If you look across the hilltops that meet the northern sky,
>  Long moving lines of rising dust your vision may descry;
>  And now the wind, an instant, tears the cloudy veil aside,
>  And floats aloft our spangled flag in glory and in pride.

*And wagons in the sunlight gleam, and bands brave*
*music pour.*
*We are coming, Father Abr'am, three hundred thousand*
*more!"*

Ricketts had never revealed that he could play the banjo at the services or funerals he had officiated along the trail. There were other occasions that called for music as well; however, there were a number of skilled musicians in the Stubbs party back at the start. They were eager to play any time the wagons stopped. *There was a banjo like mine, several harmonicas, a bugle, and even a small piano. My banjo reminded me too much of the boys that died.*

The joy created by each evening concert subsided as the miles passed, hardships increased, and the death toll mounted. *The day I rode past a small piano sitting by the side of the trail was one of the saddest I remember. Scout shied at the sight of it, and nearly threw me. I stopped, got down on my knees and touched the keys. My fingers came away dusty.*

*Who would own such an instrument, and try to bring it west with him? Maybe a concert musician from New York or Boston? A young lady, accustomed to riches and finery? Is this beautiful little piano a marker for a grave, or just a symbol of too high of hopes in what's to be found in Oregon?*

He left the cemetery, remounted, and headed south toward the ridge top, seeking a higher vantage point. *I wonder what's beyond those rolling hills.* He could see other snow-capped peaks off in the distance. *A wall of opposition, just like here.*

He dismounted at a rock outcropping, walked to the highest point, sat down, and began to play and sing again.

*"We live in hard and stirring times,*
*Too sad for mirth, too rough for rhymes,*
*For songs of peace have lost their chimes,*
*And that's what's the matter!"*

He could see all the way to the Columbia River: "*The Merrimac, with heavy sway, Had made our fleet an easy prey. The Monitor got in the way, And that's what's the matter!*"

He turned so that he faced squarely into snow-covered Mount Hood. *So beautiful, standing so defiant, guarding the land of milk and honey from us. Where should I go? How will I die?*

He thought for a moment, then continued playing and singing.

> "*So health to Captain Rufus Stubbs, Us travelers know what all he's done, He's stoppin' here what he's begun…*

He was uncertain how to finish the song. When the word changes finally came to him, he was barely able to sing them. He pointed a shaking finger at Mount Hood and declared with a mighty strum:

> "*And… you're what's the matter!*"

*I may die here. I always felt God would keep me safe as a reward for my mission work among the Indians, but now I am not so sure. If my bones are to be buried under snow or water, what was the point of any of this? Lord, did you call me to Oregon to punish me for the chapel fire in Chicago? For puffing myself up as your chosen servant? Have I misunderstood your messages? Have I fallen from the path of righteousness?*

"Where are you, God?!" he shouted.

It was then that he noticed haze off in the distance. He shielded his eyes to study it. "Smoke?" His eyes widened. He remounted and cantered toward it, mesmerized. When he failed to gain on it, he forced Scout into a gallop. He pressed on recklessly before he realized he had left his banjo behind.

"*Dust devil, I guess. A mirage. Perfect. Will I ever learn? No message in that, or was there?*

He turned back, and tried to retrace his path to the rock outcropping, the vantage point from where he started. He searched until sunset, but was unable to find the spot again. His banjo was lost.

*You have stripped me bare, Lord. Like Job in the Scriptures, you have taken everything I cherish. A final test of faith? Is Mount Hood where you intend to test me even more, or let me perish, or answer my prayer?*

He rode back to The Dalles. He realized that he no longer had any interest in preaching or in leading any kind of a revival service in the town. *It is not the things I see that I fear, but the dangers I know await me on that mountain, that I can't see. I'll take my chances by land rather than water.*

# CHAPTER 9

# A New Understanding

*Sunday October 14 1869*

Well after midnight, Virgil stood anxiously outside her wagon, and called from the darkness: "Miss Claire?"

Claire awoke with a start. "What?! Who's out there this time of night?" She was uncertain who was calling her name.

"It's me, Miss Claire."

She raised her lamp.

Her nightgown, which was too large for her, drooped and dragged on the cold wooden planks that made a rough floor. She threw her shawl around her shoulders, pulled back the canvas flap that covered the rear of her wagon, and peered out into the darkness.

"Miss Claire!" Virgil called again. "I come t' ask ya fer yer hand again, Miss Claire, an' to tell ya again that I cain't swim an' that's why I cain't go down th' river with ya to th' valley, an' I'm leavin' fer Wyomin' tonight if you won't have me, an' I won't see ya 'r ask ya again, an' I'm sorry 'bout yer stock that died from eatin' th' arrow grass, an' you losin' yer parents on th' trail an' all, an' all that's wrong between us... an' I never fired a single minnie ball at no Union boys on account of I was never given a gun. An' you're th' only woman I'm ever a-gonna love. Now I've said it. I just come t' ask ya, an' to say good-bye again iffen yuh won't have me."

"Virgil? What are you trying to say? It's so late!" She held out her lamp into the darkness. "Is something wrong? What's happened? Why are you leaving in the middle of the night?" Her heart beat rapidly in her chest. "I can't see you. Come into the light." She held the lamp out the back of the wagon, moving it from side to side, trying to find him. "You woke me up," she added, annoyed.

Virgil walked slowly into view. Claire's eyes caught a reflection from a campfire of the revolver in the holster. *He's worn that empty holster every day since he found it, until today, and now he has a gun. Something has happened.*

"I see someone's given you a gun," she said pointing at his holster. "What is going on?" Feeling faint, she abruptly disappeared behind the flap of canvas. She sat down and tried to compose herself, as Virgil stood silently outside.

"What do you want, calling so late?" She held her breath while she waited for him to speak. *I did want him to ask me again someday. But not here, not now.*

"I come callin' without an invite, 'cause you might wanna write me. I'm goin' away, gonna change my name to Palmer, like them that died."

Claire rose to her feet and threw back the wagon flap. "What? Wait! Slow down. Why are you changing your name?" She stood peering into the darkness, holding the lantern high, barely managing to discern his profile.

At the sight of her, her silhouette outlined by a combination of moonlight and lamplight, Virgil eyed her unabashedly. *She's so gol-durned purdy.*

"Stop staring at me!" she snapped. "What will people think?" She looked around to see if anyone was nearby.

Virgil turned his back as he explained: "I'm changin' it 'cause I need a proper northern name, an' I got a land deed now that says it, the names of th' Palmers, them we buried."

"You stole it off the dead?"

"No! Cap'n Stubbs give it to me when 'e left. I guess they give it to him. The Palmers, they don't have any other kin." *I hope that ain't no lie,* he thought.

"Virgil, men from our wagon train came here looking for the both of you. They think the deed was stolen. Is that why they are looking for you? What will they think if you're caught with it?"

"I done nothin'," he protested.

"There was a rumor about the Captain not returning the property to the next of kin like he promised, but I never believed it."

Virgil felt a lump rise in his throat, and he stepped back into the darkness, now afraid he would be seen by other members of the wagon train. "I was hopin' we c'd talk," he softly said. "I know I'm younger'n you. That never mattered in th' meadow that day outside Farewell Bend."

"I want an older man," Claire sharply replied. "If you were a year or two older, maybe we could court, but you are just too young. Anyway, since you're going to Wyoming, I have something for you."

Virgil heard only that there was still a chance they could be together if he could make himself older. "I carved our initials on th' back of my holster, 'member? I gotta wear it fer pertection now. Cap'n Stubbs gave me his Schofield. He left, 'cause he's afraid he'll get hung."

Claire held her lamp out into the darkness again, and glanced around. Most of the campfires were out, and the familiar smell of damp wood from water-doused fires hung low to the ground. "No one's going to hang the Captain. Come closer and hold this lamp. I found these winter boots in town." She handed him the lamp and dropped the boots to the ground. "Maybe you won't need them now, since you're going to Wyoming. Or maybe they will come in handy there."

He retrieved them, returned her lamp to her and leaned against the wagon for balance while trying them on.

"I have another gift for you, too," she said, disappearing back into her wagon. She emerged a moment later. "This pocket watch belonged to my father, and I'd like you to have it. It doesn't work anymore. I think the big spring on the winding stem is broken. Papa had a picture taken of me before we left Independence, see? It's inside here." Claire held the watch up, and moonlight reflected off the metal. "I wore my new bonnet and my mother's dress. Father said I looked quite beautiful. Not like I do now; I look like a beanpole."

"Not to me," Virgil asserted.

The watch slipped from Claire's grasp. "Oh, no!"

Virgil caught the lengthy chain in mid-air, but not before the glass face of the watch struck a metal barrel ring on the outside of the wagon.

"The glass on th' face has a crack now, but not over yer pitcher," Virgil said. "Not my fault, this time, fer once!"

"No. Dropping the watch was my fault. It's all been my fault, Virgil, not yours. I planned to leave the boots and the watch with the Captain, since I said no to you and hurt your feelings so badly. But I couldn't find him. And since you came by, I want you to have them now, to remember the good things about me."

"Th' meadow?" he asked.

"All right. The meadow, if you want. Why won't you take no for an answer?"

Virgil said nothing.

"You walked all this way with no shoes. How do your feet feel, wearing boots?"

"Stiff. These boots want breakin' in. Feels like I been shod."

Claire turned the wick of the lamp as low as it would go, without going out, despite the trembling in her hands. She thought about the message it would send to him by letting it go out completely; a final indication that her answer would always be no. *It's time to tell him the other thing that makes me wary,* she thought.

"I c'd be a-waitin' at Fort Vancouver, next spring, whenever ya get there, off the river, iffen that'd be a proper time, to ask ya again."

"I might still say no. Are you thinking of going on to the valley, then, instead of Wyoming? Most of our people have decided to wait here until the water goes down and more rafts can get up the river."

Claire took a deep breath, and changed the subject: "You should leave now." Worrying that she was delaying his departure, her words sounded sharp with urgency. She forced herself to speak more calmly: "We could meet up, I guess. The gamble is up to you. Before you decide, I need to know if you're old enough to stand on your own, apart from your uncle, and if you will be a man who can support a wife without looking to him for answers. You walk in his shadow like a puppy dog. I know he's like a father to you, but you have to decide who has your heart."

Her words were a surprise to him.

"If you go back east we won't be married, ever," she continued. "I can't wait for you to grow up; I'm twenty-five already. Your uncle was the one who interrupted us in that beautiful place. Remember? If you're going to always try to please him, if you're always going to be his little shadow, you might as well go to your Wyoming property and forget about me."

"I might never see'm again ever," Virgil said with sadness. Tears filled his eyes, and his voice broke. "I didn't know any of y'all knew we were kin, 'r that ya felt that way. He's all th' family I got."

"This is not about the Captain any longer, Virgil," she said, letting out an impatient breath. "It's about *you* and *me*—if there is ever going to be such a thing."

"It's you an' me then. Just you an' me, forever an' always," he said abruptly, surprised at how quickly he had made up his mind, his passion for her fueling his thoughts. The words had escaped his lips as if something inside had pushed them out.

Claire stared at him. She had never known him to be so decisive about anything, from the day they first met in Independence. *Will you ruin me for all other men, Virgil Stubbs?* "We might both die before we ever get to see the Willamette Valley anyway." *God forgive me for even thinking about marrying a younger man.*

"Yer th' only woman I'm ever never a-gonna want," he said forcefully. "I'm gonna prove it. We're a-gonna be th' strongest party makin' those last hunnert miles."

"I didn't know you couldn't swim," she said, with tender caring in her voice. Suddenly, she blurted out: "Can you get us over the mountain?"

Her change of heart charged him with elation. Her words thrilled him, making him feel invincible. *I still gotta chance here!*

"I'm purely sure of just one thing. We hafta leave tonight."

"Water Bess and Tillie good, then, and bring them from the pasture. I'll get the wagon ready," she replied. "Be quiet about it," she added in a whisper.

"I done put 'em in harness already," Virgil said proudly. "Didn't give 'em water, though."

"But you didn't know what I might say." She gave him a sly look, and smiled.

"Them oxen been left in th' harness overnight before. I was gamblin' I could convince ya. Cap'n Stubbs an' th' Rev' both told me t' ask ya again—had t' mean somethin.'"

# CHAPTER 10

# A New Trail

H E STOOD OUTSIDE HER WAGON AND KNOCKED IMPATIENTLY on the tailgate, fearing she had fallen asleep. "I've watered Bess an' Tilly," he whispered, "like we talked. They're fed 'n ready t' go. These boots feel fine, too. I just love ya, Miss Claire. How 'bout a kiss fer luck, now? I don't care who sees."

Claire had decided to wear her travel dress over her nightgown. She threw a shawl over her shoulders, twirled her long single braid into a bun, and forced her feet back into her stiff leather shoes.

She pulled away the canvas flap and stood in the back of the wagon, trying to determine if she had left any tasks undone. When she raised the lamp, Virgil looked up and commented: "You look diff'rent, like ya gained weight 'r somethin.'"

"Virgil, Virgil, Virgil, never tell a woman that! I put my dress on over my nightgown, silly. I've decided that I'll drive the wagon for now. I think you should hide inside until we're out of camp. Now swing the tongue so we can hitch the team. I've got to turn us around."

She bent down to reach him. The kiss that followed was full and warm. She suppressed a squeal of delight as he pulled her down from the wagon and held her fast. "We're not married yet!" she declared, finally breaking away, her eyes wide with surprise at how good his lips felt, and at how comfortable she was in his arms.

To get the oxen to back up in the dark, Claire commanded: "Back, Bess! Back, Tillie!" At the unexpected disturbance, lamps turned up full in the wagons to both sides of Claire's. The back of her wagon hit the tongue of the next wagon in the tight circle, jostling it; however, instead of angry shouts of protest, she heard only silence as she maneuvered her team forward in a turn. She held her breath. At any moment, a fellow traveler might block her path and demand an explanation. In that case, she realized that Virgil would have to make a run for it.

Luckily, most of the company slept on despite the commotion. They had endured worse: A buffalo stampede that nearly destroyed the camp shortly before they reached Farewell Bend, and the noisy arrivals of newborns, human and animal, that always seemed to occur after dark.

Claire clicked her tongue, and the oxen moved out, with Virgil hiding in the back of the wagon. She abruptly brought the wagon to a stop at the sight of a bright light. She clicked her tongue again, realizing that the lamp being swung back and forth at the edge of the circle was signaling the way out. *Someone must have overheard our conversation. I guess this means whoever it is approves of the match.* She urged the oxen forward toward the light.

Neither Claire nor Virgil found out until later that Reverend Donald Ricketts held the lamp.

Claire drove for an hour before being relieved by Virgil, and they made steady progress, stopping occasionally and briefly to rest the team. At mid-day, several horse-drawn wagon teams unknown to them caught up with them, and passed them easily. Virgil's hand rested firmly on the Schofield until they were out of sight. He observed that both teams were being driven hard. *Not from our group. Betcha they're latecomers, tryin' t' beat it over th' pass.*

Claire and Virgil crossed the Deschutes River at Dufur, and reached Tygh Valley by nightfall. When they reached White River, Claire handed Virgil several coins, and he reluctantly paid the first toll along the Barlow Road. "We come this far, we shouldn't hafta pay nothin.' Don't seem right t' me," he grumbled.

They arrived in Maupin by noon the next day, the easiest part of the trip over the Barlow Road behind them.

They found out that a number of families from other wagon trains would be spending the winter in Maupin, rather than try to traverse the pass, which was rumored to be nearly completely snowbound. Only a few units were pushing on over the mountain, and Virgil and Claire were delighted to see that among them was a couple they knew well: Willard Clark and his wife Phyllis, accompanied by Molly Mae Tucker. They had not stopped in The Dalles, and had no idea of the trouble Virgil was in.

A joyous reunion took place at the edge of town outside Toll Station Number Two, where the wagons were lined up waiting for the toll keeper to appear to collect the fee for passage to the next station, eighteen miles away.

The Clarks had arrived the day before, had purchased a second horse-drawn wagon, and were in the midst of dividing their belongings between the two conveyances to ease the pull over the mountain for both teams of horses, with Phyllis driving the second team.

Claire spotted the young girl first. "Molly Mae!" she called.

"Luck o' the Irish is with us!" Molly Mae yelled back, waving excitedly. "Are you going over mountain with us?"

Claire pointed at Mount Hood with a sweeping gesture, and Molly Mae clapped and grinned with enthusiasm.

Virgil and Willard slapped each other on the back, and agreed to head into town to gather supplies, leaving the women to help each other prepare for the trek that lay ahead. They heard, everywhere they went, about the risks of crossing the Barlow Road so late in the year, and decided to returned to the station to keep their place in line. When they arrived, the toll keeper still had not returned to his post.

# PART III

# CHAPTER 11

# Maupin

**M**AUPIN WAS ESTABLISHED NEAR THE BASE OF THE FIRST uphill incline into the foothills of Mount Hood. Shadows descended by early afternoon, a daily reminder of the mountain's ominous presence.

A bustling town, storefronts opened during the season of wagon train activity, closed earlier each day as the number of travelers slowed in the fall, and shut down during the winter.

Maupin offered the last chance to lighten the wagons of non-essentials that had value, and the travelers found that almost any item was useful while bartering for needed supplies and parts for the wagons. Warm clothing was always in demand, and just as important, rope. Those who had gold were tendered substantial discounts.

Discards often included the latest hope-chest fashions. Carried all the way from the east, but useless here, their only value was what they were deemed to be worth to trade for materials to help get over the mountain. The confections often reappeared for sale in one of the storefronts on the same day they were exchanged for something far more utilitarian.

As a crossroad for miners on their way east to Baker and to the newly discovered gold fields in other parts of Oregon, the town had grown steadily. Main Street was given over in its entirety to lively commerce.

A map of the Barlow Road was pinned to the door of Toll Station Number Two, located at the edge of town.

"To pass beyond this point, another partial payment toward the total fee of two dollars and fifty cents is due," Claire said. Molly stood beside her, while Virgil and Willard Clark looked over her shoulders.

The women read on down the posting as the men carefully studied the map. Virgil voiced what all were thinking: "This won't be easy."

Several horse-drawn wagon teams pulled out of line with impatience and moved on by, declaring to all they would pay double at the next toll station. They were moving out on their own rather than waiting to form a train, the occupants unwilling to travel with anyone they were unfamiliar with, and determined to not join forces with anyone who might hold them back.

"We follow the White River, cross near the headwaters, and proceed up Barlow Creek to the summit, the crest of the Cascade Range," Willard summarized. "The trees have blaze marks about eight feet off the ground. That means the snow may be…"

"What?" Virgil asked.

"It means the snow may get that deep."

"Never been in nothin' like that," Virgil muttered.

A soft but deep cough, which she tried to suppress, came from Claire. She had been trying her best to cover her coughs, hoping that neither of the men would hear.

"Says here, traffic goes both ways. Whoever we meet can tell us what's up ahead," Molly Mae added, trying to add a note of cheerfulness.

After reading the poster on the door, Virgil stayed with the stock and wagons while the rest of the party entered the station. A pot-bellied stove stood in the middle of the room, which contained a simple desk, a spittoon, a table, and single chair. An unmade narrow bed with a straw mattress was in the corner. The room reeked of stale alcohol. Several piles of coins were clearly in view. Other impatient travelers had paid and left, assuming the fee was the same as at White River.

Phyllis spotted a note on the rough-hewn desk, which directed travelers to the saloon down the street. She took Willard's arm, and they walked rapidly to the tavern, an unpainted decrepit shack. A slovenly man in dirty clothing slouched by the door.

"Ya lookin' fer the toll keeper? Well, this be me!"

Willard put several coins in the man's outstretched hand. "Passage for three teams. You're a disgrace. Let's go, Phyllis." The couple turned to leave.

"Wait, just wait!" the toll keeper yelled. Words slurred between hiccups, he wheedled: "Dear lady an' sir, will one o' ya take this six bits y' paid me inside an' give it to th' barkeep? Asshole won't let me back inside 'til I pay sumfun' offen ma bill."

"Certainly not!" Phyllis replied. "I'm not letting my husband in that den of ill repute!" She turned to walk away, nose in the air. The toll keeper fumbled in his vest pocket and produced three wooden tokens.

"Damn," he mumbled. "Here, Mister. You'll need these to show you paid." *Hiccup.* He threw them sloppily in Willard's direction. "Howard's a good comp'ny man up thar—stickler at nummer three station on up th' road there 'bout twenty miles. Turns 'em back, yup, at th' point of a gun iffen they try t' sneak on by.

"I bin all th' way over, mysel', once 'r mebbe twice—seasons run to… together—air's a might thin up here in th' high… {*hiccup*} country."

"It's plenty thick right here," Willard replied dryly.

# CHAPTER 12

# Twists and Turns

THE PARTY LEFT TOWN, EASILY FOLLOWING THE WHEEL RUTS of the teams that had gone on before. Stands of tall pine and fir trees gave way to deciduous aspen and maple. After five miles of travel, patches of snow began to appear in the shaded areas on and off the road.

When they stopped to rest the stock, Willard drew Virgil aside. "Why do you suppose they call that last place on the map the Devil's Backbone?"

"Not gonna be our fav'rite place, I reckon," Virgil replied.

The road zigzagged around boulders and downed trees. The familiar shades of the fall colors of New England, yellows, reds, greens, and oranges, reminded Claire of her home back east.

Just after noon, they caught up with a line of other wagons that had been forced to stop time and again. The men would unhitch a team of horses, harness one horse, and use it to pull a downed tree out of the road. Once the tree was out of the way, the harness was removed from the horse, the team re-hitched, and the train would get underway again, losing valuable time with each incident.

Joining the group by taking up the rear, Virgil and Willard walked forward while Claire, Phyllis, and Molly Mae held the teams. The two men returned with news. "They're leadin' the stock down th' canyon switchbacks one at a time and a-lettin' the wagons down with ropes."

"River's high with run-off," Willard added. "First wagon across turned over. We seen it. We'll rope our three together to make sure they don't drift on downstream."

Claire, nodded, covering her mouth. *Cough, cough.*

When their turn came, Virgil and Willard had already unhitched the teams and were prepared to lead the animals down the steep canyon. The women readied ropes, using a seaman's knot Molly Mae's father had taught her on board the Natchez Queen.

The process took several hours, but went off without mishap. The opposite side of White River Canyon was steep, and the horses, mules, oxen, and wagons ahead of them had churned up the snow and mud, filling the wheel ruts and making footing difficult. "It's like walking through chocolate pudding!" Molly Mae joked, trying to make light of the situation. "I had it every Saturday night aboard the Queen!"

They arrived at the small community of White River just before dark, to the sound of angry shouts.

"We need to stay together!"

"We ain't waitin' on you slowpokes! Those of us who had the good sense to buy stronger teams are goin' on ahead in the morning!"

"Oh, no you don't. An' let yer mangy stock eat all th' hay at toll stations three, four an' five, too! Nothin' doin'!"

"Yeah? We-all paid, an' paid good, fer our share o' th' feed."

Virgil was ready to wade into the argument. Claire took his arm, holding him back. "Only a few more days," she whispered. "Hold your tongue. I don't think there was anything here when the first wagons arrived. Look at this place." She shook her head. "There's not even any dry wood for a fire. No one lives here this time of year. Find some willow boughs to feed the stock."

Willard expressed concern over the lack of provisions, telling Virgil: "When we get higher up, if there's nothing for the stock to eat, we're in trouble. I've got eight horses to feed. If they're too weak to pull, I'll have to go back down. I'll go on ahead in the morning with the faster teams and set aside whatever food I can find for all our stock."

Willard glanced at Claire. "Never seen a woman so fond of a pair of oxen as your Claire is. She treats her Bess and Tillie like pets. You're a lucky man, Virgil, to have such a kind-hearted woman."

The next morning, very little conversation took place while the wagons were readied for travel. Once underway, the teams spread out over several miles, Willard's two wagons among them. The faster horses forced their ways around the slower mule teams, turning the trek into a race to the top. Several teams arrived at Toll Station Number Three by mid-day, paid the toll, and kept going.

A light snow fell, filling the wheel ruts, making seeing the road difficult. Each passing wagon packed the snow down, giving the pace advantage to the slower teams; notwithstanding, Claire's oxen were struggling to keep up in the rarified air of the higher altitude. They fell ever farther behind the other teams, as Claire took no chances with the well-being of her stock, and stopped every half hour to give her team a rest.

The sun made a brief appearance, brightening the moods of old and young.

"I can see the Pacific!" Molly Mae shouted from up ahead. Laughter echoed from wagon to wagon as occupants craned their necks in vain, on the off chance that the ocean was really in sight.

The higher they climbed, the colder the air. Portions of the road not exposed to the afternoon sun turned to a bumpy sheet of ice, on which the pulling stock struggled to gain footing.

Sun in their eyes, and overburdened, one of the lead mule teams sat down and refused to move. Another team tried to get around them on the narrow road. When that team tried to jump over a downed tree that lay along the edge of the road, both lead mules slipped on the ice. One fell against the downed tree, gravely injured.

A shot rang out. *Boom!* The owner had hastily put the mule down rather than let it suffer.

Claire brought her team to a halt while Virgil ran ahead. Angry shouts were directed at the unfortunate owner. "Get a move on! If we don't make number three by dark, we'll end up camping out in the open and we'll have to leave the stock in their harnesses!"

The snow was coming down harder. A team of horses was unhitched, and rehitched in front of the mules to pull the wagon off the narrow road. The horses did not like being harnessed with the mules. Efforts to control their kicking were futile, so another mule team was brought forward to replace the horses.

Suddenly, the squeal of frightened horses filled the air. Those sounds were followed by two gunshots: *Boom! Boom!* Virgil swallowed hard and struggled forward, doing his best to walk in the wheel ruts in the icy road.

Around a sharp corner and off to the side was a familiar wagon, nose-down and barely visible in a juniper trap, a large bare spot at the base of a tree that had been sheltered from the snow. Two horses, still in harness, bucked wildly. Both lead horses lay nearby, each with a broken leg, shot by the owner, Willard Clark. The contents of the wagon were scattered across the road.

On a downed tree, a child sat, sobbing loudly, her face covered with blood. Molly Mae knelt in the snow next to her, wiping the blood away with her skirt.

Phyllis stood nearby, holding the reins of the two remaining horses of one team, and the reins of the other wagon. Both teams had been startled so badly by the accident and the sound of the gunshots, they were frantic. Phyllis tried desperately to keep the thrashing hooves away from Willard, who knelt in the snow, working feverishly to cut the dead horses loose from the others. Several wagons had found a way around the blocked road; none of the occupants stopped to help the Clarks.

Claire left her wagon and struggled forward through the snow and ice to help Molly Mae with the bleeding child. *The snow is as unforgiving as the rattlesnakes on the plains,* she thought.

She bent over the child. Molly Mae looked up with pleading eyes. "I can't get the bleeding stopped!" Claire took over. She quickly and efficiently fashioned her scarf into a large bandage, and returned the frightened child to her mother.

That night, the slower teams that had been blocked were forced to make camp in the road. A single campfire was built, and everyone gathered around it, taking turns turning front-to-back to receive the warmth provided by the few sticks of dry wood that were found.

"We should be a-makin' ten miles or more ever' day and we're not a-doin' it." The man held up his hand as several men raised their hands to add to the discussion. "Hear me out. I'm splittin' off in th' mornin'. I bin holdin' my team back t' save 'em 'til now. I got th' strongest team here. My missus is half sick there in m' wagon an' we're overloaded now!" He pointed an accusing finger at Willard Clark. "It's your doin'! I shoulda been able t' make number three by noon today. I don't mind sayin' that you folks that didn't get fresh stock when ya had th' chance 'r causin' all the trouble."

"Wait a minute!" Willard protested. "I did get new pulling stock and a second wagon. We need every horse, every mule, oxen, and every man here working together..." His sentence went unfinished.

"I'll leave word at number three station that you're a-comin'," the man said, interrupting him. "If ya don't show, it'll be on him to do somethin' about it. I'm not riskin' another horse offa my team to yard somebody's wagon out of a juniper trap! If m' lead team comes up lame pullin' the weight I've got now, I'll be down t' four pullin' stock to reach th' valley." He sat down.

Several conversations began at once. Claire stood, moved closer, and spoke forcefully: "Don't be blaming the slower teams for your troubles," she said firmly. "We're stalled short of the toll gate," *cough, cough,* "because of the ice and downed trees. We can lash the wagons together, pull together in a single long train to make it easier for everyone."

"Not slowin' my pace to match your oxen," the man replied, shaking his head vigorously. "That's what you want, ain't it? We gotta get offa this mountain quick as we can b'fore it's too late an' we git snow bound. I hear it happens."

"There was nothin' for the stock to eat at White River," Virgil added. "So there's nothin' to say number three station'll have any feed. And, if there is some, nothin' says there'll be any left when we get there."

"Now look here," the man replied angrily. "I'm doin' my part. I'll keep a-carryin' some of the Clarks' belongin's, since they lost a whole wagon. He's got six horses t' my four. He can stay back with you slower teams. Lash to him. If you don't like it, look at it this-a way. Someone's gotta go fer help."

His comments were met with silence, until Claire spoke up again: "We've always been stronger when the wagons stay together."

Another woman stood up, nodding agreement, shaking her finger at the man. "You were the one needing help crossing the Snake River, remember? There was no talk of leaving us *then*!"

Those that were present at that event nodded.

"Send out a single rider on horseback. That makes th' most sense!" Virgil suggested. "But if y'all leave us, I hope y' find a suitable reward in th' valley," he added sarcastically. In the heat of the moment, his southern drawl returned

"Or in heaven," Claire added.

After a long discussion, Willard and Phyllis reluctantly agreed they had no choice but to leave with the faster teams in order to secure some of the feed, if there was any at Station Number Three, for Claire's oxen.

The next morning, the cold air was punctuated with loud commotion; shouts mixed with whinnies echoed up and down the road as the hungry teams were readied for travel before daylight. No one wanted to be last in line, as they would be the most likely to be delayed further.

By mid-morning, the usual time for departure, Claire, Virgil and Molly Mae found themselves alone on the road in a silent world, a white wonderland of trees so heavily laden with snow, they bent low over the road. Claire had offered to let Molly Mae ride with them, so the Clarks could keep up with the faster wagons.

The squeak of the metal fasteners that hooked the single tree and yoke to their wagon seemed out of place in the stillness; the sounds echoed across the expanse of rolling white. Virgil harnessed the team of oxen, and the trio got underway, with Molly Mae on the front seat of Claire's wagon holding the reins, Claire and Virgil walking along on either side.

Their encouraging words to the two oxen were the only sounds: "On Bess, on Tillie." They took turns with the chant to keep the oxen pulling forward. After another snowfall overnight, the oxen were pulling through drifts up to their knees anytime the wagon jumped out of the wheel ruts.

Molly Mae was silent. The shock of seeing the child's blood dripping in the snow haunted her. She stared straight ahead, huddled under a blanket, her expressionless face streaked with tears, holding on to the reins. No matter what Claire said to her, she refused to utter a word.

The wagon wheels occasionally broke through the ice-covered wheel ruts, making forward motion ever more difficult. The constant strain forced the oxen to stop frequently. By midafternoon, dark shadows blanketed the forest floor. Virgil knew they were miles behind the Clarks. There was no sign of Station Number Three.

Claire knew she had a fever, and wanted to keep it from Virgil. *He has enough to worry about.*

The still mountain air carried the sound of the crack of an occasional whip from somewhere up ahead, echoing down the road toward them.

"I wonder if Willard will leave the station before we even get there!"

"You would think the choicest land is reserved for the fastest team down the mountain!" Claire replied between coughing spells. *Perhaps the road up ahead is better. I hope so.*

The two oxen were unable to avoid stepping into the wheel ruts that now ran three feet deep.

Claire grew so tired walking that she climbed up into the moving wagon to lie down in the back. Virgil, on the other side of the wagon, didn't notice her absence until he realized he was calling to the oxen by himself.

In spite of her throbbing head, Claire was determined to get Molly Mae to react. "I think the road looks like a chocolate sundae, with streaks of vanilla," she called from the back. "What do you think?" Molly Mae remained silent.

A cascade of snow fell with a loud *whump* from an overburdened tree limb that stood along the side of the road. The oxen abruptly came to a halt. Virgil urged the team, unaccustomed to snow, ice, and the rarified air, to move forward.

He heard someone cough several times, but assumed it was Molly Mae.

A few minutes later, off in the woods, a loud *crack* shattered the quiet around them, startling them, and reminding them of another familiar, sickening sound: that of a wagon axle breaking. It was the sound of another tree limb broken free, followed by a loud *thump* as both limb and snow fell to the forest floor.

As the hours passed, Claire burned with fever, and her slender body shivered. Molly Mae silently beckoned to Claire to sit beside her and share the blanket thrown around her shoulders. Claire moved back up onto the seat of the wagon, and the two huddled close. Still, Molly Mae did not speak.

Seeing the two women wrapped together for warmth made Virgil nod with satisfaction. *They've been good friends since they first met.*

# CHAPTER 13

# Howard Stall

A LONE RIDER APPEARED ON HORSEBACK, COMING TOWARD them. He trotted up to them with an authoritative air on his dark face, and raised his hand for them to stop. Virgil drew the Schofield, which the man on the horse did not expect.

"Easy, friend. I'm Howard Stall, toll keeper fer Station Number Three, up th' line there. No need fer drawin' on me."

He had closed the books for the year after the other wagons came through an hour before, certain that they were the last travelers he would have to process, or show hospitality to, for the season.

He kept an eye on Virgil's gun hand, and placed his hand on the grip of one of his six-shooters. "Nobody mentioned t' me that a slower wagon wuz still on th' road, 'specially someone so quick t' draw iron," he said. *Not a smart move t' draw like that, sonny,* Stall thought. *Yer wonderin' 'bout me, y' didn't 'spect t' see no Creole out here.*

"Weather's due fer t' git worse," he said in a low voice, as he watched Virgil's thumb hover over the hammer. *A Schofield revolver. Iffen he cocks th' pistol, I got no choice but t' defend m'self.*

He was confident he could draw, fire and drop Virgil where he stood before he knew what hit him, but as the two men faced each other, Stall was thinking about something else. *Leavin' m' post cuz of heavy snow shouldn't cost me m' job. Kill this boy an' it will, shorely enuf.*

"You folks're travelin' two ox short fer a safe crossin' this time o' year," he announced with sternness, as he dismounted and extended his hand toward Virgil. "Anyhoo, you'll hafta be turnin' loose o' that gun t' give m' hand a proper shake."

Virgil thought: *He ain't out t' hurt us.* Virgil put the Schofield back into the holster.

Claire and Molly Mae squeezed each other's hands. Claire placed a hand over her heart to calm herself. After the two men shook hands, the tension in the air dissipated.

"Ma'am," Stall said, tipping his hat. "Young lady," he nodded at Molly Mae. He dusted the snow off his hat and placed it back on his bald head. "But I'm nary an expert on th' weather," he added, with a grin and a chuckle.

"These two oxen by themselves have pulled this wagon the last five hundred miles," Claire announced with pride.

"That's mighty fine. Y'all expectin' t' catch up to that bunch up ahead yonder?" Rather than wait for an answer, Stall turned back up the road. "I ain't never seen a string o' wagons so anxious to see th' ocean. I come 'round th' horn in sixty-four, meself, during th' war," he said. "Wisht' I'da come overland like you smart folks; I was sick th' whole way!" His smile was infectious, and had, no doubt, helped him land the job in the harsh wilderness on the southern slope of Mount Hood.

"You in th' war, then?" Virgil asked.

"Fer a time," Stall replied, turning back to Virgil. "Fer a time. Yew-Ess-Army treated me good! I'ma thinkin' 'bout joinin' up again next year. I wuz in Andersonville Prison, in Georgia, 'til some of us broke out."

Virgil nodded and swallowed hard.

"Oregon's a free state, but a Creole man's almost like a black man, cain't own land out here like I kin back home. Go figure. We was here first, too. You serve in the cause o' Lincoln, son?" he asked. "Drummer, mebbe?"

Virgil looked at Claire. "Too young," she replied.

"Jus' wanted t' thank ye, iffen y'did." Stall smiled again.

He bent over to check his horse's cinch. *I could let 'em pass through fer free. They won't find much at the station, 'cept straw in th' mattress that they kin use fer food fer th' stock. We lose a few keepers ever' year, they jest run off.* He turned around, eyeing the Schofield revolver, making sure it stayed in Virgil's holster. He bit his lip, deep in thought. *I gotta sweeten this up fer 'em. Allus good bus'ness.*

"Yer toll t'day covers passage west 'til ya git t' Number Four Station. But I'll be proud t' lead ya back down the mountain t' Maupin, fer free, iffen you's of a mind t' turn around."

"We're a-goin' on to th' valley," Virgil announced decisively.

"Suit yerself. In that case, th' toll fer passin' through is two bits a head. Make it an even half-dollar fer th' lot o' y'all. Only two more stations after mine. Cain't say there's much at any of 'em, 'cept a roof over yer head. Y'all kin stay th' night inside up yonder, 'bout a mile up th' road. Follow th' blazes on th' trees iffen m' tracks're covered up. Iffen ya don't, ya might miss it. Cain't say I left much fodder, after them other folks come through. Should be some straw under th' floor, I use it fer m' beddin'." He chuckled. "Never seen a bunch so eager to get down th' mountain. Me, I like th' snow."

Claire's cold fingers struggled with the pull-strings on her purse. She handed some coins to Stall.

"When ya git to th' station, look in a li'l tin can on th' top shelf over th' stove. Tokens're in there. Ya gotta be able t' prove ya paid me!"

Stall remounted, eager to be on his way. *Not my job t' discourage,* he thought. He smacked his lips at his horse and his obedient sorrel broke into a brisk walk.

He had said nothing about the narrow steep ice chutes at Laurel Hill or about the ridge above the Sandy River known as the Devil's Backbone.

"Th' road is here t' serve th' fever, Oregon fever," Stall mumbled to himself, as he trotted away. Part way down the road, he scowled, stopped, turned his horse back the other way, and rode back to the wagon. "Blazed trees're down up ahead, make sure ya don't miss th' station. It be on th' right." Tipping his hat at the ladies, he left the lone wagon and headed east.

Stall planned to spend his winter in another state. Not all of the money he had collected over the summer was entered in his business books, a strategy he had followed for the past two years. *Army never paid me fer more'n a year whilst I was in prison.*

*This comp'ny don't pay shit neither. They give less ever' year fer cuttin' wood, fixin' the road, an' dolin' out th' fodder. More 'n more goin' east these days than west, too.* He urged the sorrel into a trot.

*A hot bath, new clothes, an' female comp'ny fer th' next month! Hit's what I got in mind, paid fer in part by H an' H Sterling, th' current owner of th' Barlow Road.* Searching for the right words, he shook the snow off his hat again and said out loud: "rec-nition… Sterling don't give no rec-nition— fer th' wood cuttin', fer takin' th' money, an' fer keepin' th' books all summer."

He thought about his encounter with Virgil. *Now, me offerin' a smile an' handshake 'stead of a bullet, gotta be worth a raise next year; me jest bein' friendly kept his hand away from that Schofield.* He stopped his horse in the middle of the road and turned it back toward his toll station. *I swan, there's just somethin' about that boy. Like prob'ly-so I seen 'im b'fore…* The thought vanished. He bowed low, his strong thighs keeping him from falling from the saddle. "Thank ye, thank y'all." He put his hat back on his head and squeezed his legs against his horse's flanks, signaling the horse to trot.

*Them that's got th' fever gotta be numb with cold t' cross this time of year. Try tellin' 'em 'bout what's up ahead, try tellin' 'em 'bout th' weather. They're determined t' go on—I kin always spot their fever.*

*A good comp'ny man does right by his employer no matter what. Shoulda mentioned t'other thing—them wolves hangin' 'round th' station. I wonder did that kid ever even fired that Schofield? I wonder do he ever even know how to load it?*

Accustomed to talking to himself during the long periods of isolation at his toll station, he asked himself a question, and then answered: "Should I stay on th' Clear Water over th' winter? Yes, you say? Yes, then!"

Stall hoped to avoid running into anyone who had crossed in either direction this time of year, unless they offered a card game. *Cain't refuse that,* he thought. *Don't hafta let on who I work fer. Th' Clear Water'll be a fine li'l winter place fer me.*

104

He had heard rumors that angry miners had demanded their money back on their journey going east over the road; they complained that the road was nearly impassable. When the toll keeper at Station Number Four had refused to issue a refund, the miners had beaten him senseless. *Don't need nobody beatin' me to a pulp over things I cain't do nothin' about.*

*Funny thing, Oregon a free state, but a man like me, even with m' light skin, cain't own land like them folks; land grabbers all of 'em. No credit fer fightin' in th' war neither. Jest don't seem right.*

A large clump of snow from an overhanging tree dropped to the ground with a loud *whump!* directly in front of him. Buck reared wildly, dumping Stall. He landed seat first in the soft snow, still holding onto his horse's reins, a trick he had taught himself years ago. Not holding onto his horse had once meant he had to walk for miles in the desert sun.

He laughed. "Ha! Softest landin' I ever had!" He stood up and looked back down the road. *There be somethin' familiar...* The same memory returned. *I know that boy. I seen him b'fore. I'm purely certain. In Georgia.*

The memory came to him in a flash. *It was outside Savannah, Georgia, on th' Stubbs plantation, where m' daddy worked in th' fields 'cause he was a dark skinned black, 'n m' momma were th' nursemaid fer th' kids 'cause she was Creole, so they let her in th' house.* "He was a-sittin' on the mastah's lap, yessir." *Mastah Stubbs was one hard man, 'n swift with th' whip. If th' boy's here, mebbe ol' mastah is too? On'y one way t' find out. T' make things even, I'd be willin' to give up m' job.* He fingered the Colt that hung loosely at his hip. "Judge Colt an' his jury of six'll sort things out."

He turned his horse and signaled him into a canter, heading back toward his station. *'Cept he was jest only a boy back then, an' he's tryin' t' be a man now.* Just as impulsively, he changed his mind again and stopped. *War's over fer both of us. Nothin' like a warm fire in Maupin. This old man's on th' way to th' Clear Water. Ain't gonna fight no losin' battles, no sir.*

Not far from the place in the road where Stall had left the party, Claire's wagon slid into the ruts left by previous wagon trains and hit bottom with a jolt, nearly throwing both women off the seat. Wheels now up to the axles in snow, the oxen stopped. The threesome pushed the wagon from the rear, with all their combined strength, to get it moving again.

"He might have killed you…" Claire exclaimed, breathless.

"But he didn't," Virgil replied. "Funny thing, seein' a colored man, a-ridin' down this road like he owned it. I sure didn't expect t' meet up. Imagine that, him workin' a job up here."

"Maybe it's the only one he could get," Claire suggested. "Did your family ever own slaves, Virgil?"

"No. We was poor. Cap'n Stubbs did, though. Sold 'em off b'fore th' Yankees got near Savannah. Some runned away, I guess, an' joined the war. He never let on how many. Cap'n came out here 'cause he lost it all. He wants a fresh start now in Montana. He's bound 'n determined t' own land again. When y' own land, ya make th' rules."

"That Mister Stall probably came for the same reason," Claire said.

Molly Mae turned, and gave Virgil a long look. "Why did you come, Mister Virgil? To get rich? To own land?" she asked.

*She's finally talking again*, Claire thought with elation.

"Never figgered I had anything t' lose, bein' with th' Cap'n. He's my uncle, ya know. Nothin' t' lose 'til I got here, that is—'til I met Miss Claire."

Claire smiled.

"An' these boots, I'd hate t' lose 'em," he added with a teasing smile. "First ones I ever owned."

Virgil was more vigilant than he appeared. "Y'all see that blaze mark on that there tree?" He pointed at a tree by the side of the road with a cleanly cut notch three feet off the ground, proud that he had spotted it first. "Right there!" He pointed. "Snow's gotta be four feet deep alongside th' road! Road's packed purdy good. No way t' stay outta th' wheel ruts."

# CHAPTER 14

# Number Three Station

L OCATED STRATEGICALLY AT THE TOP OF BARLOW PASS, Number Three Station was situated for good visibility to detect approaching wagons coming from either direction. A thick alpine forest surrounded it on all sides. To bypass the station was impossible. A traveler attempting to avoid paying the next toll installment by skirting the station would have to cut his way through the forest first.

Claire sank up to her knees in snow as she helped Molly Mae step down from the wagon. Together they struggled onto the porch of the log structure. It took both their efforts to force the weather-swollen door open. Claire smiled at Molly Mae, pleased that the girl was talking again. "Let's see what we can find," she said.

To Claire's surprise, Molly Mae began singing softly to herself as she poked at the dying embers in the pot-bellied stove in the drafty cabin.

"I'm glad Mister Stall didn't put the fire out or put a lock on the door." *Cough, cough, cough.*

"Your cough is getting worse."

Claire nodded as she held her hand over her mouth, as if doing so could prevent the next round of coughing. Her throat burned with pain, and she could feel herself growing weaker.

Virgil unhitched the oxen from the wagon, and tethered Bess and Tillie inside the protection of the three-sided loafing shed attached to the station. The oxen pawed hungrily at the snow in search of anything edible.

Virgil searched under the cabin floor, startling a pack rat that scurried out and disappeared. He found an armful of straw and gave it to the oxen. *Don't smell too bad,* he thought. He dusted the snow off a small woodpile with a gloved hand, the gloves another gift from Claire, and filled his arms with as much wood as he could carry. He headed inside, confident that he had done all he could for Bess and Tillie. *Someday we'll have our own place. I'll learn to farm, just like Capt'n Stubbs, an' she'll keep house.* He smelled beans cooking and biscuits baking as he leaned his weight against the stubborn door to open it.

After enjoying the hot meal, the trio turned in early. Molly Mae and Claire climbed up a series of slats nailed to the wall, and slept on the toll keeper's narrow cot in the loft. Virgil wrapped himself in a pile of moth-eaten blankets and curled himself around the stove. The wind howled most of the night, and they awoke to discover that drifting snow had piled up against the door.

They decided to rest the stock until noon, giving Virgil time to scout the road ahead. After struggling for what he estimated was a mile across a nearly flat and open ice field, he returned with troubling news.

The three stood around the stove, Virgil rubbing his hands vigorously to warm them. "Near as I c'n tell, any blaze-marked trees're buried under th' snow. I ain't sure which way th' road goes across the ice field up ahead."

"Can't you find the wheel ruts?" Claire asked.

"It's all packed ice up there. Most o' the snow's blown away by th' wind. We sh'd leave soon's I warm up. I just gotta find the way — where we start across, an' where we need t' end up on 'tother side. If we get off in that soft snow, Bess 'n Tillie won't be able t' pull us a'tall. Cain't say what's underneath neither—what they might step into."

There was silence for more than a minute. Claire spoke up, trying to brighten the mood. "I know you can get us down off the mountain, Virgil. We're almost there. We'll all tell stories about this, some day."

Freezing vapor clouds formed in front of the oxen, obscuring their vision, as they stood, waiting to begin the journey toward the ice field. Virgil chummed the oxen forward with a handful of bunch grass he had found buried in the snow.

They traveled halfway to the ice field without difficulty, but the oxen brought the wagon to an abrupt stop on their own in front of a downed tree, laying squarely across the road.

"I didn't see this. It musta' just come down." Virgil saw that the metal strips that covered the wooden wheels of the wagon were coated, packed with a mixture of mud, snow and ice. "The wheels hafta be cleared b'fore we c'n find a way to pass around th' tree," he announced. "Some of it comes off easy." He kicked one of the wheels with his booted foot.

Claire and Molly Mae went to work on the other side of the wagon, using a tree limb to poke at the packed ice. Claire shivered with cold, and started coughing non-stop. *Cough! Cough…*

With a shovel he had taken from Station Number Three, Virgil poked down through the snow, searching for the wheel ruts. What he uncovered was a blazed marked tree that had fallen. "We're still on th' road!" he yelled with excitement.

They got underway again. "On, Bess, on, Tillie!" Virgil urged repeatedly. The beasts required more coaxing; the blowing snow landing on their nostrils and in their eyes making them pause and lower their heads.

Claire laid down in the wagon, trying to regain some strength. Virgil heard her uncontrollable coughing. He brought the team to a stop, and rushed to the back of the wagon. "You hafta ride an' take'er easy th' rest o' th' day," he commanded. "An' cover up good. You must be freezin'."

"It's more than that, Virgil."

They both heard Molly Mae singing softly:"Whatever my lot, thou hast taught me to say,It is well, it is well, with my soul."

Virgil looked as if for the first time at Claire's angelic face, now so pale, but ethereally beautiful. He gazed deeply into her emerald green eyes, took her soft little hands in his big rough ones, and forced himself to give her a big grin."We're gonna make it, Claire. Y'know, I just purely love you."

Claire smiled and nodded.

"Back to it!" Virgil whooped with what he hoped sounded like enthusiasm.

He realized that the blazed trees marked only one side of the road. If they were to drift out onto the wrong side, they could be going the right direction, but making travel through the heavy, unpacked snow nearly impossible for the oxen. They could easily drop into a juniper trap.

He hurried ahead to locate the next marked tree to keep them moving on the right side, leaving the wagon behind.

Claire said to Molly Mae: "I know Virgil wants me to stay lying down, but I've got to do my part while I can." She stepped down from the wagon and walked ahead of the oxen, following Virgil's footsteps, hopeful that he was leading them in the right direction. "On, Tilly, on Bess," she said, her voice pleading with her trusted oxen not to give up. The obedient beasts trudged on. Claire began to cough almost continuously. *Cough...cough...cough.*

Virgil was unable to find the next marked tree. He walked in what he thought was a half-circle to see if the trail turned left or right. He lost his balance several times in the soft snow that so effectively disguised the rough terrain.

*I thought I knew where we was; that ice field hasta be here. There 'tis!* He stood at the edge of the ice field and looked across. *I hafta find th' road on t'other side 'fore we try t' go across. How'm I a-gonna do that? Gotta go back to th' wagon. Tie m'self to it. Gotta tether m'self so I won't stray too far.*

When he turned back his footprints were no longer visible. Snow began falling hard, turning within seconds into a blinding storm, disorienting him. He was uncertain which way to go. He heard Claire coughing violently, the wagon much closer than he realized. The words of the hymn Molly Mae sang resonated as if they were hanging in the air, and he shouted: "Is it well with you?"

"It is well, husband," came her reply. Virgil felt invincible and very mature; her assurance that they would one day be married a welcome confirmation.

*Does she want t' pertend we're already married? Mebbe she said it fer th' girl's benefit. There's lots I don't know, but now I purely understand what that hymn's all about.*

Claire greeted him with a hug and handed him a long rope, which he wrapped around his waist and tied. Tethered to the wagon now, he set out again and struggled through waist-deep snow in an arc, searching for the one tree he was sure he could recognize again, that marked the starting point across the ice field. He pulled the length of rope behind. *It has to be here somewhere.*

"It is well!" Virgil yelled from the left. The road had turned sharply and he had nearly missed it.

"It is well!"Claire yelled back repeatedly, between coughs, as loud as she could.

"With my soul,"Virgil called weakly. He felt a tug on the rope. Claire was pulling him back to the wagon.

"With my soul!" Claire repeated. *"Cough! Cough!"*

Something stronger than the tight rope squeezed against his sides, but he felt no desire to resist the stricture. He wondered if feeling Claire tugging on the rope gave him confidence, or if he was numb and disoriented from the cold.

*Am I freezin' t' death?* From a place deep inside, a flurry of unbidden thoughts surged through him. Virgil felt conflicted and confused. He was losing a battle, one he didn't know he had been fighting. A shower of awareness of his humanity was overpowering his childlike wariness—his sense of weakness —his feelings of inadequacy.

*I feel like I'm dying, but it's like I'm bein' reborned too. It's a feelin' a man c'd give in to.* He knew he wanted to get back to Claire, that her presence would make him whole. *I c'n go hand over hand. She's holdin' on. She understands.*

Without him realizing it, a newness had been growing inside, perhaps for months—ignored, as he had ignored the pricks, pains, and gouges to his bare feet as he walked across the prairie. *I reckon I been a-growin', but was I growin' into somethin' good or bad?* Virgil didn't know.

Then consciousness surged over him like a warm blanket and came to the surface. For the first time in his life, he formed what he felt deep inside into words. "I called myself a man, but I wasn't. I belong t' Claire, an' we belong t'gether. She loves me like a woman oughtta but I'm purely jest still a-learnin' how to be a man. This here rope might's well be her arms around me, an' what ropes us t'gether is strong as th' feelin's Uncle Stubbs has fer th' land." He felt the comfort of her presence, as if she was standing next to him, and he could see the loving look on her face.

Virgil stood motionless in the newness of growing into manhood, no longer worried about who he was, who he was trying to be, nor who he would become as Claire's husband. He strained his eyes to look through the snowflakes that stuck to his eyelashes and beyond the canopy of trees overhead, as if his smiling face and open mouth exposed all his senses. He saw as if for the first time the forest-green boughs covered in white and the patches of blue sky that allowed the sun's rays to make shadows on the forest floor.

Her voice brought him back to the moment: "It is well!" Claire shouted. *"Cough! Cough!"*

"With my soul," he boomed the reply. *We're strong together.*

With the starting point of the narrow road across finally clear, Virgil was still uncertain where they needed to end up on the other side. He ventured out two more times, stretching the rope as far as he could, then untying himself, but careful to keep the bearing tree in sight. There was a sheer drop-off on both sides, and going farther meant losing sight of the tree around which he had tied the rope.

With shadows in the dense forest growing longer, in near white-out conditions, Virgil acknowledged that they would have to wait for the snow to stop. No forward movement could be gained in what remained of the day. He reluctantly returned to the wagon.

The trio set up camp, and ate a cold and meager meal. Virgil threw a canvas tarp over the oxen, cleared the snow from around their feet to try to help them stay warm, and gave them the last of the straw he had brought from the station. Virgil, Claire, and Mollie

Mae huddled together for warmth through the night in the back of the wagon. Claire's coughing finally subsided and she drifted into a fitful sleep a few hours before daybreak.

The next morning, snow was still falling, and the trio's hope for an early start vanished. The wagon was frozen solidly in the ice. They decided to leave it, walk back to the station, and wait for better weather. They unhitched the team, and returned to the cabin, leading the docile oxen, loaded with the few belongings they thought essential.

Two days before, no one had taken charge as the wagons that had left Virgil behind attempted to cross that same barren ice field. Willard Clark's wagon was last in line, and the Clarks watched in horror as ice and inexperience coupled in disaster. The drivers of two of the wagon teams tried to avoid the wheel ruts cut deep in the ice, and both wagons slid sideways, jerking the pulling stock of horses and mules with them. The drivers whipped the teams hard, trying to right the wagons, but to no avail. The wagons picked up speed as they slid down the steep slope. Occupants of the wagons jumped to safety in the nick of time, but nothing could be done to save the stock or wagons. The horses panicked. One fell, then another, pulling others down with them. They spun out of control as they descended down the steep slope of the ice field and out of sight. A sickening crash was heard from down below, followed by screams of pain from the stock. Other than a broken arm, none of the travelers was hurt, but the injured stock had to be shot. The drivers of the remaining wagons refused to attempt to cross the ice field until a workable plan was proposed; in the meantime, what could be salvaged from the wrecked wagons was carried back uphill and distributed among the remaining wagons.

Willard Clark came up with a plan that the others quickly approved. The teams were unhitched. Stout ropes, lengths of chain, and harness leather were tied together and stretched across the ice field. The horses, moving in a single file, pulled one wagon across the expanse of ice, using the wheel ruts as a track. A second rope was fastened to the back of the wagon, wrapped around a tree, and let out as the wagon was pulled across, preventing any further slides down the hill. Willard assigned himself to hold the back line around a nearby tree, and to hold it taut, insuring that the wagon being transported did not drift out of the shallow wheel ruts. When signaled that the rope was tight in front, he slowly let out the back line.

When all the wagons were safely across, Willard waved to Phyllis, and shouted: "Stay with the others!" He had been thinking about Virgil and Claire, and realized that they would not be able to cross the ice field without help. He decided to ride back toward Station Number Three in search of them. When he saw the abandoned wagon, he knew they were in trouble, and he urged his horse on, through the deep snow, to the little cabin.

He arrived at the station, tethered his horse in the loafing shed and stepped on the porch, stomping his feet to clear the snow from his boots. The commotion outside brought Virgil promptly to the door. He forced it open, the worry on his face evident to Willard. Before Willard could speak, Virgil said, "Ya come back, 'n thank y'all! We're stuck here. Where's ever'body?"

"They went on to Laurel Hill. My wagon, too. I come back to warn you. You can't cross the ice field alone. You go to be tied front and back to keep you in the wheel ruts."

"Our wagon's stuck in the snow. Can you help free it?" Claire called weakly from the loft.

"Yes, but it won't do you any good. I can help you pull your wagon back down here, but I can't stay with you after that. I think the best thing for you to do is to stay here. I'll go for help. You stay here and wait for a rescue party.

"I brought you some food; it's in my saddlebags. The only piece of good news is that it's downhill most of the way after you get across the ice field."

"Why don't we cross now, use yer horse an' th' oxes on neither end t' hold th' lines tight?" Virgil asked.

"Because we're short of rope. The backline ropes we tied together still stretch across all right and we can use it in front to pull you across. It's frayed bad in places, but it could work. But unless you're carrying two hundred yards of stout rope for the back line, your best chance is to stay put 'til help arrives, whether from the government camp or from folks in the valley. The ice is a solid sheet, and once a wagon starts to slip, there's no way to stop it."

"We cain't stay here. Iff'n we do, we'll starve!"

"Not if I can help it, Virgil," Willard said with authority. "I'll make sure the arrangements are made. You have my word. You know how close we are to the rivers. We're close to Oregon City, and everything. Can't be more than ten, twenty miles away. You could walk it if you had to!"

"My Claire's come down sick. She cain't walk that far. But both women c'd be doubled up on yer horses, 'n *you* c'd walk!"

"That won't work, Virgil, and you know it. One slip, and we're all finished."

"What choice do we got? Molly Mae sh'd go with you, then. She c'n walk across that ice field."

A faint voice was heard from the loft: "Then we can go… to America. Papa's going to try, try… farming there." Virgil rapidly climbed up to the loft, and was shocked at Claire's appearance. She was incoherent, her face flushed and wet with sweat, and she burned with fever. *I gotta get her down offen this mountain! We hafta find a doctor.*

Molly Mae scurried up the ladder's slats with a clean cloth she had doused in the water pail. She handed the cloth to Virgil, who took it and gently wiped Claire's forehead. "I want to stay with Claire," she announced. "I can nurse her, Mister Virgil."

Virgil's mind raced. *Iffen I try to move her, that'll kill her, I'm purely sure. I dasn't let her git cold. We gotta stay put, and just hope help'll come.*

# CHAPTER 15

# A Raw Hunger

WILLARD ROSE EARLY, AND HANDED THE SADDLEBAGS THAT contained the basic provisions he had been able to pack to Virgil. "Make it last as best you can, son."

"If'n we run out?"

Willard motioned for Virgil to follow him outside. Neither man spoke as they trudged through the snow to the loafing shed. Virgil threw the saddle blanket over Willard's horse, and Willard followed with the stiff leather saddle. After he tightened the cinch, he mounted and pointed at the oxen. Not a man of many words under the best of circumstances, Clark was unable to speak.

"Claire'd skin me alive if'n I did."

Willard nodded, shook Virgil's hand in a fond gesture of farewell, and reluctantly set out, wishing he did not have to leave the young and unexperienced trio alone. His thoughts were soon diverted: His horse reared, trying to avoid walking into the deep snow, and Willard was forced to dismount and lead the horse toward the ice field.

Claire's fever broke an hour later, and she insisted on seeing her oxen. Leaning on Molly Mae's arm for support, the two struggled a few feet past the front door and stopped. Claire did not have the strength to go farther.

A shot rang out. *BOOM!*

"Virgil?!" Claire cried.

She forced her feet to take a few more steps. From the corner of the station, she could see only one of her oxen. Alarmed, she called: "Virgil! Where are you?"

Virgil appeared from behind the shed.

"I only see Tillie! What were you shooting at?" Claire did not see the man standing next to Virgil.

"Mountain lion, I think. Big cat of some kind!" Virgil replied. "It's gone now! Go back inside."

"Find Bess!" she demanded.

"Go back inside, now!" he yelled again. Trembling with shock, he could not bear to tell her what had happened to her other ox.

Only an hour before, he had stood on the porch with unwelcome tears in his eyes, watching Willard leave. A commotion at the back of the station made him curious. *Prob'ly just snow slidin' offa th' roof, but I better check 'n make sure.*

He approached the loafing shed with caution, his hand on the Schofield. He saw that only one of the oxen was in the shed. The sound of breaking tree branches in the surrounding woods caught his attention, and he noticed blood-streaked marks leading from the shed off into the trees.

Virgil's heart raced in his chest. *I gotta find Bess!* He followed the blood trail through the heavy snow into the nearby woods, fearful and alert. *Gotta be a bear! Nothin' else c'n take down an ox like that.* The path was easy to follow; signs of a struggle were evident in the snow.

Whatever it was, Bess had been forced to the ground, and had been dragged off into the trees. *But Willard an' me were just standin' here!*

The attack by the wolf pack was strategic and timely. Their target was the oxen with the shortest horns, the one less able to defend itself against the pack. They had sat silently in the woods and waited for the opportune moment. Once the two men walked away, the temporary delay in their attack was over.

The crimson stains on the fresh-fallen snow were mixed with large patches of hide that had been brutally ripped away. The wolves were after fresh meat.

Virgil's heart sank when he came across the steaming remains of Bess. Her carcass, now hardly recognizable, had been torn into portions and dragged into the woods in two directions. *Bears?* Virgil's anger surged. He cocked the revolver and plunged deeper into the woods. *I got five shots an' I'm gonna use all of 'em if I hafta!*

117

He chose the largest blood trail and headed that direction. He caught up with two adult wolves and two half-grown pups, all feeding greedily on the fresh meat. He raised the revolver, pointed it at the largest wolf, and pulled the trigger. *Click! A misfire.* One of the wolves raised his head and then returned to feed, unconcerned, ignoring Virgil. Two more cartridges misfired. *Click! Click!*

The wolf turned Virgil's way again, and bared blood-stained teeth, unafraid, annoyed at the intrusion.

Virgil realized he could be taken down even more easily than Bess, and fear replaced his anger. He backed slowly away, his hand shaking as he continued to point the revolver at the wolf. *If they attack I got two shots left; if both misfire, I'm a goner.*

Darting from one tree to another, using them as cover, he got to what he judged was a safe distance, and then turned and ran for all he was worth, headed for the station, fearing that at any moment he would be taken down from behind and killed by the pack. He fell several times in the deep snow, and struggled quickly back to his feet. *My only hope is to get inside the station!*

When he was twenty yards from the station, he was terrified by the sight of an enormous mountain lion jumping on Tillie's back. He raised the Schofield and pulled the trigger. *I might hit Tillie!* The revolver misfired again. *Click, click.*

A mighty *boom!* resounded from somewhere nearby. The shot echoed off the trees and Virgil jumped, startled and uncertain where the shot had come from. "*Yeooww!*" The mountain lion screamed loudly and limped into the forest, leaving a trail of blood behind.

Virgil turned in a circle, looking for Willard Clark, thinking he had returned and fired his rife at the huge cat. Instead, Howard Stall stepped out from the shadows.

"I fergot t' mention 'bout them wolves. I was a-watchin' you make a run fer it in th' woods there. Had you covered with m' Colt, best handgun ever made. This cat was a surprise, though. Big fella. Spoiled his breakfast, didn't I?" Stall chuckled. He waved his gun in the direction of the drops of blood that led off into the trees. "I better go find him an' finish the job. Blood trail shouldn't be hard t' follow in th' snow."

"Thanks," Virgil stammered.

"Hadn't seen him before. No siree. You, on t'other hand, you, I mighta seen down Georgia way. That possible? If so, you's a long way fr'm home, Georgia boy."

Virgil froze. *Is he a relative of one of Uncle Stubbs's former slaves? Jesus, help me!*

Stall didn't wait for Virgil to answer. "I hear mountain cat tastes like pork. You hear diff'rent?"

"No, Mister Stall. No, t' both yer questions. I never heard nothin' 'bout what a mountain cat tasted like. An' we ain't met b'fore. Me an' Elizabeth are from Indiana."

"The li'l girl is kin, then?"

"No, ridin' with us 'cause her wagon fell in a juniper trap an' broke an axle."

*I saw it,* Stall thought to himself. *That part of the story is good.* "If you've a mind to help me with the skinnin', before them wolves pick up th' scent, I'd be obliged."

Virgil nodded. "Okay," he said hesitantly.

Stall reloaded his Colt and followed the crimson trail into the trees. A minute later, Virgil heard the cat screech again: *"yeowww,"* followed by another *boom!* from Stall's gun.

Virgil stood next to Tillie, stroking her face, his mind racing. *Bess is gone. We got no way to pull th' wagon now. An' Stall... why'd he come back?*

Stall's return interrupted his thoughts. "All part o' th' service here on th' Barlow Road, friend," Stall yelled, walking back into view, dragging the carcass behind him. "When we're finished here, I aim t' git you t' th' next toll station. I'll be collectin' th' toll fer th' rest o' th' road, once we get there. I know number four's empty, mebbe number five too. We don't see many wagons this time o' year. You kin slide on yer backside all t'e way t' Rhododendron from number four station."

Stall's next question sent a chill down Virgil's spine: "I never got yore name?"

Virgil thought fast. *I gotta tell Claire we hafta start usin' our new names right here. He's just gotta swaller whatever story I feed 'im. I cain't defend m'self. Danged gun don't do nothin' but misfire, ever' gol-durned cartridge. Gotta stick to m' story, gotta make 'im believe me!*

"Verin, Verin Palmer, Mister Stall," Virgil replied cautiously. "Kin t' Gen'ral William Jackson Palmer of Pennsylvania. Gotta Wyoming land deed that says so," he added defensively. "We'd appreciate yer help. Cain't pull th' wagon now with only one ox. With Cl...what with Eliz'beth ailin', we're in a fix."

"You shorely are, son. You shorely are," Stall replied, as he dropped the carcass between them. "Let's string the cat up in th' shed here an' git t' skinnin'. Nothin' like fresh flour-coated meat fried in bacon grease!" He clapped his hands together, and then clapped Virgil on the shoulder. "Right, son!?"

Virgil couldn't take his eyes off Stall's Colt. "Right," he said weakly. *Gun looks like it gits a lotta time outta th' holster.*

At that moment, the two women appeared at the corner of the station. Claire called out: "Virgil!"

"Mister Stall come back," Virgil replied. *Stall will be suspicious now.* "He shot that big cat in th' nick o' time...Eliz'beth. I, uh, I couldn't find Bess," he lied, rubbing his hands together to restore warmth to them. "We're doin' th' skinnin' now. Go back inside b'fore you take worse!"

Turning to Stall, he spoke rapidly: "She calls me usin' her Pa's name whenever she come down with th' fever. She thinks she's back home in Ireland, but her family come over 'n settled in Indiana whenever she was just a li'l bitty thing. We 'preciate you helpin' us git to th' next station. There's s'posed t' be a rescue party comin' t' git us offa th' mountain. I'll be back quick as I git the women back inside."

Molly Mae looked at Virgil suspiciously, and started to question him. He raised his hand to hush her. "Jest wait 'til later. Back inside now, both o' you," he repeated. Claire's knees buckled. Virgil grabbed her around the waist, and with Molly's help, guided her back inside and carried her up the slats that led to the loft.

Virgil whispered in Molly Mae's ear: "I be Verin Palmer now, and Claire be Elizabeth Palmer, fer Mister Stall's benefit, y' hear? We're husband an' wife. Y' understand?"

Molly Mae frowned and nodded. "But…?"

"No buts," Virgil said sternly. Our lives prob'ly depend on it."

Molly Mae's blue eyes grew wide with curiosity, but she nodded her compliance.

Later that day, Virgil broke the news about the ox to Claire, who had stayed in bed all day, weak, coughing, and unable to eat or drink. He tried to comfort her, but she turned away from him, sobbing, shoulders shaking with despair. Molly Mae sat on the bed beside Claire, and tried to console her.

Claire turned to Virgil and burst out: "Bring Tillie inside tonight and Mister Stall's horse, too. I'm not letting them stay out there to be attacked again." Her sudden lucidity was a surprise and made both Virgil and Molly Mae hopeful that she would recover.

Howard Stall had occupied the cabin every season for several years, and was unaccustomed to having visitors stay for more than a few hours, especially three persons accompanied by a full-grown ox and his horse, but he infused the situation with his typical good humor. Swishing tails slapped faces and knocked over the table that held his horse's saddle and the station's only lamp. Molly Mae and Claire took refuge in the loft. "My station's bigger'n t'others. Good thing!" he chuckled, shaking his head and grinning widely.

Constructed of rough-cut boards, which Stall had planed over time, the planks extended overhead the width of the cabin, but not the length. The wooden floor of the loft came to an abrupt and ragged end, leaving a gap of some three feet. Molly Mae sat there as she ate her meal, dangling her legs over the edge.

Supper was steaks Stall cut from the mountain lion, along with some dried vegetables he produced from a root cellar.

Conversation during the meal was sparse. Stall abruptly asked: "Are you kin t' Joel Palmer of Pennsylvania, by any chance? He helped build this road back in forty-five."

"Never heard'a him," Virgil answered, swallowing hard.

"Just askin'." He sat at the table and rocked back and forth, playing his harmonica and doing his best to avoid both swishing tails and eight very heavy hooves.

Molly Mae recognized the tune and sang along from her perch in the loft:

> *"Jesus loves the little children,*
> *All the children of the world.*
> *Red, brown, yellow, black and white,*
> *All are precious in His sight.*
> *Jesus loves the little children of the world."*

"It's a prisoner's song," Stall announced. "Got diff'rent words fer me than what you sung. Learned it in Andersonville Prison durin' th' war." He sang the same melody, with the words he heard from other convicts:

> *"Tramp, tramp, tramp, the boys are marching,*
> *Cheer up, comrades, they will come,*
> *And beneath the starry flag*
> *We shall breathe the air again,*
> *Of the free land in our own beloved home."*

Virgil pressed against the door frame, trying to avoid the hooves and horns attached to two very large animals in a much-too-small space. He maintained a nervous silence, trying to distract himself from his swirling thoughts by watching Tillie and Buck eat the straw from Claire's mattress that Molly Mae threw down from above as she talked about her life on the Natchez Queen.

"I allus wanted t' ride in one o' them floating palaces all th' way to N'Yawlins, like a big spender," Stall exclaimed. He clapped his knee with joy. "An' right here in m' station I got someone who done it! An' you lived on board th' riverboat. If that don't beat all!" He shook his head with delight. "Once in m' lifetime. Once in m' lifetime, I'm gonna do it."

Stall was full of stories, especially about his time at the station. Despite worrying over Claire's worsening illness, the rest of the evening was filled with laughter, most of it coming from the toll keeper.

The cabin was warm, and all slept soundly that night, humans and the huge beasts, in spite of the cramped conditions. At dawn, Virgil and Howard patiently and firmly returned the animals to the loafing shed. Virgil and Molly Mae then went to work on the cabin's interior, using a mixture of melted snow, lye soap and ashes to remove the offal.

Stall produced a stash of beans and flour he had buried in a metal box beneath another floorboard in the station. Along with the meat provided by the mountain lion, they had food for several more days.

Claire had slept well and awoke feeling refreshed, but within a few hours, the fever returned with a vengeance. She was unable to sit up to eat, so Molly Mae held her head while Virgil tenderly fed her water and broth, a few drops at a time. She alternately slept fitfully and talked incoherently. When her fever finally broke again, she sat up, and was able to drink some warm broth on her own. She felt well enough to comment on the savory aroma from the boiling broth on the stove that filled the station.

Just before sunset, the wolves returned. Howls resounded from every direction. Tillie and Stall's horse Buck were again brought inside. "Took th' cat's entrails a ways off but they no doubt finished those an' smell th' animals inside here, and us too." Stall checked his supply of ammunition. "Nobody goes to th' outhouse unless I go too," he ordered.

Claire fell into a deep sleep.

*I am sixteen and we are moving again so Papa can find a more profitable farm. I am not big and strong enough to swing the scythe.*

*I know he is disappointed that I can't be more help. I try hard but I can't fell stalks of wheat, and I'm no good at shocking corn. All the farmer boys are away fighting in the war. There is no one but me and Mama to help Papa.*

*We grow corn. It is tall, over my head. I try to help, but I get so tired! Papa is talking about moving again, maybe finding a farm where he can raise beef or hogs this time. We have lived in Indiana, Minnesota, and Iowa. I guess now we are headed for Missouri. We are always moving farther west, toward Oregon, because Papa wants to end up there, eventually.*

The next morning, after the animals were moved to the loafing shed, and the cabin cleaned as thoroughly as possible, Stall prepared breakfast, but did not linger over the meal. He threw the saddle outside onto the porch, and motioned for Virgil to follow him. Stall spoke quietly as he bridled Buck: "I changed m' mind 'bout all us leavin' t'gether. Yer woman needs t' stay inside where it's warm, an' she needs tendin'. I know the road on down th' grade. I'll git them wolves t' foller me. An' I'll send help back to fetch ya."

"How you gonna do that, Mister Stall?" Virgil asked.

"I'll drag the cat hide behind me. That, an' fresh droppin's from Buck, should keep 'em thinkin' they're chasin' a wounded animal. I should be able t' catch t'other bunch o' travelers. They'll hafta lower th' wagons down on ropes through th' Laurel Hill Chutes. That'll take sev'ral days. An' they still got t' cross th' Backbone above th' Sandy River. You got any more rounds for th' Schofield?"

Virgil shook his head.

"Here, then, take one o' my Colts. I got a rifle, too. D'ya know who's in charge o' th' wagons?"

"Not nobody, Mister Stall," Virgil replied.

"Call me Howard, son."

"Ask fer Willard, Willard Clark. He helped us get back down here from th' ice field. Left just b'fore you come."

"Ya said last night two wagons didn't make it 'cross th' ice field."

Virgil nodded. "They shot their horses that slid with th' wagon an' left 'em lay, down at th' bottom, I reckon."

Howard shook his head and drew a deep breath. "No wonder th' wolves an' that cat hung 'round here. They kin smell anything dead or dying, even if th' crows don't find it first an' give it away." He motioned for Virgil to come closer, and spoke in his ear. "Iffen ya run outta food b'fore I get back…" Stall nodded toward Tillie, "ya know what y' hafta do."

Vigil swallowed hard. "I hope it don't come t' that."

Stall patted his shoulder and nodded. "Burn whatever's made o' wood t' stay warm if y' get snowed in or ya run outta bullets. I don't have anything more t' leave ya with."

Stall mounted up and clicked his teeth, giving Buck the signal to trot.

# PART IV

# CHAPTER 16

# Playing Catch-up

REVEREND RICKETTS RODE HIS HORSE SCOUT HARD UP THE Barlow Road, reaching Maupin just one day behind Claire and Virgil. He had been told by the toll keeper at White River that the last group of wagons was quite spread out along the road, and that he should easily be able to catch up with the slower-moving ox-driven teams. He also learned that several different groups were going over the mountain, some of which were members of the Stubbs party. *My people!*

He gazed up toward the cloud-covered mountain and swallowed hard. He had paid the fee, after waking up the agent who was sleeping inside Number Two Station at the edge of town.

The last establishment on the outskirts of the little town was a dry goods store, and Ricketts decided to go inside and make sure he had everything he needed.

Learning that his customer was a preacher, as he himself had once been, and that the traveling reverend was perhaps the last person passing though going west for the season, the merchant decided to get rid of as much excess inventory as possible, and make Reverend Ricketts his best-prepared customer of the year.

"Reverend, if you're crossin' the Barlow Road alone this time of year, you need to put on the *full* armor of God," he said. "Be strong in the Lord and His almighty power, 'cause you're gonna need it."

"Oh, I am, sir, I am," Reverend Ricketts exclaimed, pleased that the man was taking such an interest in his welfare.

"Is there a church in this little town?" he asked.

"Only a mission, run by the Catholics. Priest comes through from The Dalles, once a quarter."

"I may have met him," the Reverend replied. "Short man, round face?"

"That's him." The merchant launched into an often-repeated story: "I had my own church once upon a time back in Wisconsin, gave it up to save the unsaved here, but they don't much want to be saved."

Reverend Ricketts gave him a puzzled look.

"The Indians, Reverend, the Indians. Now," he exclaimed, slapping the counter with his hand, "my pulpit is this counter right here, every day, not just on Sundays. A man's got to make a living. I do the occasional wedding. The betrothed stand right there next to that pickle barrel. Oh, and here's a list of what I sell the most of to the Road People. That's what I call 'em. Road goes both ways, you know! Keeps me in business most of the year, 'til the snow flies."

After reading the list of items earlier travelers had purchased, Ricketts decided to buy everything the part-time merchant, part-time minister suggested.

"Extra food for me and grain for my horse, of course." *I'll need much bigger saddlebags.*

As if the man could read his mind, the merchant mentioned: "I just happen to have one pair of large saddlebags left."

Ricketts hesitated when the merchant insisted he buy a new Henry rifle and two boxes of ammunition. *I've never owned one. The man has an honest face and means well, I'm sure. If he thinks I need to be armed, I probably do.* He finally nodded his approval.

"This is the famous Henry .44-.40," the merchant said enthusiastically. "Best carbine on the frontier! You load it on Sunday and shoot it all week long." He handed it across the counter. "At least, that's what them Rebel boys said during the war."

The caliber numbers meant nothing to Donald. *Heavy,* he thought. *Never shot one of these. Probably kicks like a bay mule.*

"My sword of the Spirit, right?" he added, referring to the biblical passage the merchant had quoted. *The man knows the word, I'll give him that.* "I already have a scabbard, so I don't need the belt of truth, sir."

"Fair enough." The merchant nodded; his smile of satisfaction growing with each item Ricketts purchased. He neglected to mention that this model of the Henry rifle was no longer manufactured, and that this, his last remaining Henry in stock, had been passed over numerous times by more knowledgeable travelers. The biggest complaint was that the gun had no safety mechanism. Once a round was chambered, the slightest pressure on the hammer could make it fire. Its heft of ten pounds was also considered a liability among weight-load-conscious mountain travelers.

To keep Donald on a buying spree, the merchant threw in a small canvas tarp and a length of rope. "My meager gifts to you for your mission work, Father...I mean, Reverend." He moved to a rack of clothing. "This is my last oilcloth raincoat. Think of it as a way of girdin' your loins up and wearin' the breastplate of righteousness, all in one." He fit the poncho over Ricketts' head. "Now, let's find you a pair of winter boots and a hat."

"I know this one," Reverend Ricketts said excitedly, not realizing how quickly his money was being spent. "Shod my feet with..."

The merchant interrupted. "It's all preparation for you spreadin' the gospel of peace, Reverend, preparation for travel."

"And don't forget the helmet of Salvation!" Ricketts said, enjoying the exchange.

"No offense to your Padre hat there but you need one with a chin strap against the wind up thar on the mountain." *May not be many more travelers, what with the railroad goin' coast to coast. I need to push what's left on the shelves a bit harder.*

By the time the sale was concluded, Ricketts was down to his last five dollars, but he felt a renewed sense of confidence in himself, telling himself that he was well-equipped for his journey.

As soon as he left the store, the merchant put a "closed" sign in the window and locked the door.

Ricketts pounded on the window, as he realized he would need more information about the road ahead. "How far to the next toll station?" he shouted.

The merchant yelled back through the glass: "Maybe eighteen miles! You can find your way by followin' the wagon ruts of them that left day before yesterday. The same ruts've been used for years. Cut three feet deep in places, they tell me. The blaze-marked trees will guide you all the way to Oregon City, Reverend."

"What's a blaze-marked tree?"

"Out in a minute."

The merchant exited the store, giving the locked door a final tug. The conversation between the two men continued on the wooden sidewalk.

"You mean hatchet marks on the trees when you say blaze marks?"

"Yup, eight feet off the ground. Marks the roadbed when the drifts cross the road. It mostly works unless the marked trees fall down. You should make White River by noon tomorrow. A few cabins there, not much more. Nobody stays up there year 'round. Number Three Station is another ten miles beyond. After that, there are two more stations, ten miles apart. Keep a-lookin' up, Reverend. It's the only way to see the hatchet marks on the trees. We call 'em blaze marks, but don't ask me why." He quickly walked away.

Ricketts' new saddlebags were filled to overflowing. He put the rifle in the banjo scabbard. It fit perfectly. *I'd rather have my banjo.*

As he settled himself in the saddle, he looked with determination at Mount Hood, and offered a short prayer to gather his courage. Speaking to the mountain as if it could reply, he opened his Bible and read aloud the passages that he and the merchant had shared.

His horse pawed the ground, and started walking without a signal from him. When Donald finished reading, he took a deep breath and urged his horse to go faster.

He shouted at the mountain: "For we wrestle not against flesh and blood, but against principalities! Against powers, against the rulers of the darkness of this world, against spiritual wickedness in high places!"

He rose in the saddle and looked up the road as far as he could see. There was a dusting of snow ahead, and two single tracks were starkly visible. *The wagon wheel ruts are plain as day, nothing to worry about.*

A mile down the road, he reigned his horse to a stop. "We left out the shield of faith." He uttered a brief prayer in reference to the portion of the passage he had forgotten.

He rode on, deep in thought. *God will reveal his plan for me just like he did for Moses on the mountain. When one door closes, God opens another—I think...*

He put his horse into a canter and hurried up the White River Ridge, riding between the wheel ruts. He eased his horse down the slippery canyon wall and led it across the roaring headwaters, eager to get to the next toll station before dark.

The tight canopy of trees overhead blocked the sunlight by early afternoon, and seeing the road became increasingly difficult. He dismounted and walked ahead of Scout. Not only was visibility poor, but he had nearly been knocked from the saddle by low-hanging branches weighed down by snow. Relieved when several snow-covered roofs of the cabins that lined the banks of the White River came into view, he unsaddled Buck, tethered him in an open shed nearby and brought everything else inside a stale-smelling bunkhouse. *I'm prepared for anything.* He knocked on the door of every cabin, but got no response: White River was empty. He found some willow branches for Buck to eat, adding some grain from his saddlebag. He munched on heavily salted jerky, washed down with water.

The next day he walked ahead of his horse again. The wheel ruts were filled and covered over by the snow, and deep enough to cause injury should Scout step into one by accident.

He stopped at the wreckage of an abandoned wagon, nose down in a juniper trap. *Hmmm. I wonder what happened here.* He turned his face away from the partially eaten carcasses of the two dead horses shot by Willard Clark.

Late in the day, he realized he was smelling smoke. Certain that it was coming from the next toll station, he urged Scout off the road toward it, hoping he would find someone there. The snow was knee-deep, and he was quickly exhausted and remounted. He urged Scout on until he found the source of the fire. A snag, target of a recent lightning strike, was smoking, the fire burning in the roots underground.

A thin layer of pitch-scented smoke hovered overhead. The snow had melted in a perfect circle out from the base of the tree as the root system caught fire. "This could be my sign!" He dismounted and knelt down to pray, feeling with gratitude the warmth of the soil on his knees. He felt around with both hands. *Warm to the touch. Hallowed ground. Is this my burning bush!?*

He decided to retrieve his Bible and search for any mention of a tree standing upright, but burning underground. When he stood up, any notion that this was his sign vanished. He was surrounded by the same pack of wolves that had killed Claire's ox Bess at Number Three Toll Station. They had been feeding on the dead horses, and had followed him into the woods, more out of curiosity than hunger. He surreptitiously removed the rifle from the banjo scabbard.

The wolves began snarling, baring their teeth, pacing back and forth, but staying outside of the circle of warm soil, preferring the safety of the snow to the perceived danger of fire.

Impulsively, Ricketts pointed the gun at one of the wolves and pulled the trigger, but the rifle did not fire. *The merchant didn't load it and neither did I!*

He had not asked how to work the lever, either. Not being familiar with the firearm, he did not know that that action was necessary, in order to drive the hammer back to cock the carbine.

Scout was nervous, so Reverend Ricketts slowly remounted, fearful his horse would run away and leave him on foot and at the mercy of the wolves. "Easy, Scout. Easy, now," he crooned, forcing his voice to sound reassuring. The scar on his forehead throbbed and burned as he exhorted himself to stay calm.

He turned his horse in a tight circle, looking for a way to escape, reaching at the same time into the saddlebag behind him to retrieve a box of cartridges. He laid the rifle across his lap and fumbled to open the box. He removed a shell with cold fingers, but he no idea where to put it to load the carbine. He pulled the lever down, keeping one eye on the wolves, and tried to feed the shell in through the open breech.

At that moment, the largest wolf stepped into the circle, overcoming his fear of the smoke. Startled, Ricketts lost his hold on the box of ammunition. It fell it to the ground, shells scattering in all directions under the nervous horse's hooves. Several bounced against Scout's front legs and he reared, nearly throwing Donald to the ground. The horse bolted out of the circle back toward the road, jumping high over the nearest wolf. The reverend gripped the saddle horn with one hand and the Henry with the other, and as they soared over the nearest wolf, he raised the gun and yelled: "Bang!"

# CHAPTER 17

# Pioneer Woman

CLAIRE SPOKE SLOWLY AND PAINSTAKINGLY, GAPS BETWEEN her words punctuated by her struggles to breathe: "I'd like you to write some words for me, Molly Mae," *cough, cough,* "before the consumption takes me."

Virgil rushed up the slat ladder, banging his head on the low-hanging roof as he rushed to her side. "No!"

"Virgil, I know I have it—the signs, my mother had the same… I need you to wait outside. Put your jacket on…and wait outside. Please." Claire painfully choked out the appeal.

"Mister Virgil, Verin, please, do as she says."

Virgil reluctantly went outside. Claire beckoned Molly Mae to come closer. "I want you to write something for me. Don't let him read it until I've passed," she said weakly.

Molly Mae took her hand, her eyes filling with tears.

"No!" Virgil cried from outside, banging on the door.

Claire's eyes had lost their luster. She stared blankly at the split log ceiling and forced her thoughts into words. "There's a little pencil in my picture book."

"What do you want me to write?"

Claire dictated, between debilitating fits of coughing, as Molly Mae transcribed the words, in her most legible penmanship, pausing frequently to puzzle out what she hoped was the proper spelling:

*Virgil,*
*I except your pripposal of marriage today. I don't have a*
*white wedding gown like you dream about. I'm going to*
*heaven, but my heart's here with you.*
*I don't know what name should be on my marker, O'Connor,*
*Stubbs, Palmer? None seem right. If you mark the place*
*where you burry me, put this:* **Pioneer Woman.**
*Use peaces from my wagon to fit a proper coffin. I want*
*to ware my mother's dress from the trunk. The one in the*
*locket pitcher I gave you.*
*Don't visit this place again. I am not here, only my bones.*
*It is well with my soul.*
*Look after Molly Mae. Three years diffrence.*
*I love you, husband*
*Claire*

The loud knocking became a steady banging. Molly Mae hesitated before descending the slat ladder, dreading having to try to calm Virgil. She opened the door and saw two men standing there: Virgil and Reverend Donald Ricketts.

"Reverend Ricketts!" Molly Mae gasped, "You have answered our prayers." She waved him inside. From the loft, Claire's words almost imperceptibly floated down: "I want to be married *[cough, cough]* and share this bed with my husband tonight."

She strangled to choke out the words, her eyes becoming vacant pools of green. The trio crowded up the ladder to the loft with Virgil leading the way. By the time they made room for each other around the little cot, her breathing had slowed, and her expression no longer showed recognition or pain.

Virgil gently took her small white hand in his. "Claire," he said quietly, his voice not more than a whisper.

She smiled at him, her eyes suddenly bright and shining. "I do," she said.

"I do," he replied.

Her head fell back, and her breathing stopped.

"No!" Virgil cried. He threw himself across her body, sobbing. Ricketts reached around Molly Mae and gently but firmly pulled Virgil away from Claire's unresponsive body. "Let her be, now, let her be. She's passing from this life. Let her go. There is nothing more that can be done."

Molly Mae tenderly closed Claire's eyes, kissed her ashen cheek, and said: "It is well. You are well." She burst into tears.

# CHAPTER 18

# Decisions

"I cain't jest bury her and leave 'er here, Rev'rend," Virgil said through his tears. "We was almost married."

"We can't take her body with us. I think you know that," Ricketts replied.

"Them wolves might, y' know, dig 'er up."

"They'll likely stay close to the dead stock 'til everything's gone," Molly Mae sniffed. "Just like pigs around a trough."

"But they know we're here," Virgil pointed out. "They already took down one of her...our oxen. They know we're inside here. With only one ox now, we cain't even pull th' wagon nohow. We're stuck here."

"My Scout, he don't like a harness, nor snow, for that matter. I don't see harnessing yours and mine together helping our situation."

Virgil nodded, and the bereaved trio stood silently, each person deep in thought.

"You should read what Claire wrote to you, Mister ....Verin." Molly Mae hesitated, not sure whether she should be addressing him by his new name. "From last night, when she asked me to write her words down, remember? Her last words."

Virgil took a deep breath. "Well, read her words, then, bein' I'm not so good yet with letters." He sniffled.

"No, I think you should." She handed him the notebook, and Virgil slowly read the words, and then read them again. There were several he didn't know. When he pointed to them, he looked at her to fill them in.

"She said all this? This last part here, too?"

"Yes, every word. I don't know what she meant by the last part. I'm sorry." Molly Mae turned away toward the stove and sobbed. *I couldn't save you either, Claire. I'm so sorry I ever came here.*

A short distance from the station, Virgil scraped the shallow snow away near the base of a tall tree. The frozen ground eventually gave way to the shovel that he found in the loafing shed. Tears streamed down his face as he dug the grave.

After an hour, Molly Mae appeared with some broth and a biscuit for Virgil. He forced a smile, but said nothing. "These are the last of those Claire made for us the first day we arrived at the station," she said, hoping the food made with Claire's hands would somehow give him comfort.

For a moment, she stood watching him eat, waiting.

"Thank you," he said, finally.

"I've dressed her," she said, then turned and walked back to the station house.

Reverend Ricketts relieved him with the shovel work a few minutes later. Virgil looked back down the road. *How long will it be before the wolves return, I wonder?* "Are you a good shot with that rifle?"

The reverend dug stoically for a few more minutes, then stopped and leaned on the shovel. Sweat had beaded on his forehead and was dripping onto the snow. "I don't even know how to load it. I bought it in Maupin. I called it my sword of the spirit."

Virgil gave him a questioning look.

"Let me explain. Take over here a minute."

Virgil took the shovel again and slammed it into the partially frozen soil.

"A man has to gird himself up with the whole armor of God. Ephesians 6." He felt as if he was standing in a pulpit in The Dalles, making a last-ditch plea to the faithful to help the Indians. He pointed his finger at the nearby trees, as if they were members of a congregation in danger of losing their salvation. "That ye may be able to meet the evil one! The helmet of Salvation…"

"Ya got any more ammunition, Rev'rend?" Virgil broke in. "I left m' gun inside."

Ricketts was surprised at the interruption. "There's another box in my saddlebag. I lost one. Good story! The horse spooked…"

"Git yer rifle an' cartridges NOW!" Virgil shouted forcefully.

Without stopping for an explanation, Ricketts hurried away, reacting to the urgency in Virgil's voice.

Virgil felt a chill of fear as he caught a flicker of movement off in the trees. *Not fallin' snow, that's purely certain.* Whatever it was had crept to within a few yards. He backed slowly toward the station, ready to swing the shovel if he was attacked.

A large snowshoe rabbit bounded out into the open and stared at him with curiosity before lopping off into the trees.

Reverend Ricketts came puffing up behind him. "What was it, a wolf? Do we need to make a run for it?"

"Just a rabbit," Virgil sighed, limp with relief. "A critter, Rev'rend, with all the armor it needs. See them big feet and that snow-white coat? Tough t' spot, easy fer th' rabbit to make a quick get-a-way. Now, if you've a mind to finish here, I'll get to pullin' up th' floor boards. They'll suit to build a coffin."

Virgil took the rifle from Ricketts, and studied the tube-shaped spring-operated magazine. *Uncle Stubbs talked about Yankees that had something like this. Shot a bunch of times without reloading.* "Hand me them shells." He pulled the magazine tube spring open, and demonstrated how to insert the ammunition. "They go in up here, see?"

When it was loaded, Virgil handed the rifle to Ricketts. "Now, pull th' lever down. See? It's ready t' shoot. When th' hammer is way back like it 'tis now, ya pull the trigger. If y' see a wolf, just raise 'er up an' fire. Should scare it off. You got a long sword now, Rev'rend."

Ricketts held the weapon up proudly. *"Bang!"* he yelled, looking fiercely out into the trees.

Virgil shook his head and walked to the wagon. He knew Claire kept a wooden mallet in the toolbox, which was mounted on the wagon's exterior, next to a small rain barrel. *I'll reuse the nails. Seen it done b'fore.* He went to work dismantling the floorboards from underneath. *Should be building' a cabin, not a coffin.*

Tears filled his eyes again. His heart ached. *I c'd build a box big enough for th' both of us. Rev c'n take care of Molly Mae. No, Claire asked me to. Why'd she do that?*

Moonlight was reflecting off the snow around him when he finished. He heard footsteps crunching through the ice crust that had formed on top of the soft snow.

Ricketts announced: "It's finished."

"Ready here too, Rev'rend."

"In the morning I'll do the service, of course," he said as he put his hand on Virgil's shoulder. "Then we have to leave. It was her wish."

Virgil nodded. He was thinking about what was coming after the funeral. *I'll be leavin' Claire in this God-forsaken place.*

The next day, Reverend Ricketts and Molly Mae laid Claire in the grave and the two took turns filling it in. Virgil went to work building a sled, one Tillie could pull. He tied some of the remaining wood together with rawhide, and used the curved barrel staves for runners. Once loaded, he covered their belongings with a portion of the wagon canvas top.

Before beginning the burial service, the trio stood around the stove in the little cabin to warm themselves one last time. "We should have a plan in place," Reverend Ricketts said. "Shall we take turns leading the horse and the ox?" "We should stay here and wait," Molly Mae pleaded. The men seemed not to hear.

"Nobody rides the sled," Virgil replied. We tie the rope to Tillie's yoke and Buck's saddle horn. You lead Buck out front, Rev. Molly Mae you ride on Buck. Foller the rope across. If the sled starts to slide sideways, cut the rope, let it go, don't get tangled in it." "But it means losing Tillie!" Molly Mae continued to object.

"Who carries this rifle, then? It weighs a ton by itself."

"Whoever's in back sh'd carry it," Virgil suggested. "Me."

"Agreed."

"If th' wolves catch up to us, Rev'rend, you know what to do."

"What do I have to do?"

"Cut Tillie's throat with my knife."

"You can't be serious!"

"It's meat they're after." Virgil climbed the slat ladder, and busied himself throwing down armfuls of the remaining mattress straw. "This is food for Tillie and Scout. Let's jest do what we can t' keep th' animals alive, and us, too."

# CHAPTER 19

# An Odyssey on Ice

"I DON'T WANT TO LEAVE HER."

"It's time we moved on, Virgil. Or is it Verin?"

"I know, I know. Just lemme be with her a li'l while longer."

The Reverend had not asked any questions about the name change until now.

*I sh'd stay an' make sure they can't get to her in th' coffin,* Virgil said to himself.

He did not realize Molly Mae was standing behind him until she spoke. She touched his arm. "Mister Verin?"

"You c'n just call me Verin now. No need t' call me mister."

"Claire was clear about what she wanted, wasn't she?"

"Yeah."

"You've done almost everything she asked of you."

He nodded, wiped his face on his sleeve, and then looked at her with a puzzled expression. "Almost everything? What d'ya mean? Th' part 'bout takin' care of you?"

"No. Not that. I can take of myself, thank you."

"What, then?" He pulled his arm away.

She dropped a flat piece of wood from the wagon's tailgate at his feet. He looked down at it. Using charcoal from the stove, she had written the words Claire had requested: **Pioneer Woman**.

Molly Mae was crying. *I couldn't save his Claire.*

"I'm sorry," he said, trying to hold back his own tears. "Let me do th' rest." He used the mallet to drive a nail through the marker and into the closest tree.

"Claire trusted me t' get her to th' valley an' I failed," he said, when he had finished the sad task.

"I tried to nurse her, and I failed," she replied. "You've no need to tend to me. Once we're off this mountain, I'll find my own way.

I'm as grown up as you."

He was stunned by her show of independence. He had always thought of her as a child. Pulling a small knife from his belt, he traced the letters Molly Mae had carefully drawn, carving over the words: **Pioneer Woman**.

Meanwhile, Molly Mae took the shovel, filling it with snow and rocks, and packing the materials on top of the dirt.

The trio gathered around the fresh mound, which looked painfully out of place in the expanse of snow.

"Accept the soul of your servant, Claire Louise O'Connor," the reverend began, hands clasped together. He looked at Virgil, uncertain which name to add to his prayer. "She was a fine…"

"Pioneer woman," Virgil and Molly Mae said in unison.

"She was a fine pioneer woman, betrothed to Mister Verin Palmer, here. Almighty God, protect us all for what lies ahead. Amen."

Virgil looked around for the last time, hoping to commit to memory the location of Claire's grave. *Hundred feet east from the station, under this fir tree.*

Virgil and Molly Mae went inside the cabin to gather their few belongings and to make certain they left the temporary refuge as neat as possible. Virgil climbed into the loft one last time to visit the last place he had seen Claire alive. The little space was nearly bare: the small cot, a few articles of clothing, a worn satchel… Virgil spotted Claire's sketchbook on the floor under the bed. He tucked it inside his shirt and descended the slat ladder. Taking one last look around, he gazed back up at the loft. *She said yes up thar.*

Ricketts was outside, practicing aiming the rifle, when it suddenly discharged with a loud *Boom!*

"Jesus, Rev'rend! What're ya shootin' at?" Virgil yelled as he raced outside.

"Thing went off on its own, I didn't do nothing. Well, I might of bumped the hammer. Doesn't seem to have a safety." He scratched his head with surprise.

"Keep it pointed t'other way!" Virgil commanded, more frightened than angry. "Sorry 'bout takin' th' Lord's name in vain," he contritely added.

"Forgiven, Verin. You should take the rifle now, before we start across the ice field up yonder." He handed the rifle to Virgil and Virgil handed him his knife and sheath. Donald looked at it and swallowed hard.

Tillie effortlessly pulled the lightweight sled carrying their few possessions up the slope toward the ice field. The trio looked across the open expanse, observing that the field narrowed near the far side with drop-offs on both sides. The wind blew in their faces, and snow began to fall again. Reverend Ricketts plunged forward, head bowed, leading Scout into the storm. Molly Mae hunched over in the saddle.

"Lissen up!" Virgil yelled over the howling wind. "If y'all hear me shootin', keep goin', don't look back! If they're trailin' us, I cain't hold 'em off forever. Double up on th' horse, an' go as fast as y' can. I'll try t' catch up! I'll leave th' last shot fer m'self!" His final words were lost in the howl of the storm.

"You can't just leave Tillie, she's defenseless!" Molly Mae yelled back.

"It's meat they want. The Rev'rend's horse'll be next. Then us, if we cain't get offa this mountain!"

"Lord, protect us," Ricketts pleaded, as he plunged forward again. *Do you intend to take everything from us and leave us like your servant Job? Are we destined to freeze or to be eaten by wild beasts?*

Moments later, shots resounded across the ice field: *Boom, Deada! Boom, Deada! Boom, Deada!* The shots came in rapid succession, echoing off the mountains. Ricketts broke into a run, pulling his nervous horse behind him. Slipping and stumbling on the ice, he did not notice that Molly Mae was no longer in the saddle.

Donald heard a number of additional shots, and discerned that the muzzle sounds changed to those of a sharper, less powerful blast. *He's stopped using my Henry?*

Upon hearing the first shot, Molly Mae made her decision. *I'm not leaving you, Verin! My mother left me, my father left me, your uncle Stubbs left you, and your Claire left you. I won't!*

Out of breath in the thin mountain air, the reverend stopped, afraid to look back. *Something's wrong. The Henry holds 'way more bullets than I heard.* The smell of the approaching wolf pack, combined with the noise of gun shots were making Scout difficult to control. "Easy, boy!" he shouted repeatedly.

It was then he discovered that Molly Mae was no longer on Scout's back. *Oh, my God! She must have fallen off!* He looked anxiously back into the howling storm. Scout unexpectedly reared breaking the frayed rope, pulled free from his grasp, and disappeared into the storm, running toward the trees on the far side of the ice field.

*Do I run after the horse, save myself, or go back and look for the girl?* He felt drawn back across the ice field toward the sound of the gunshots, now coming in rapid succession from the Colt revolver Howard Stall had left with Virgil. *There has to be something I can do.* He fought off his fear and tried to pray. *On the other side, the wolves are waiting.* The wind at his back pushed him forward, hurrying him to traverse the final yards across the open ice field. *If this is my fate, then I will perish here.* He found himself counting the steps. *Ten more steps. Can't be more than eight now, six, four, two. Got to find them!*

He did not see blood on the ice, nor any trace of Molly Mae's clothing; he saw no tracks of footsteps. *Did she slide down one side? Why didn't she yell to me? Would I have heard her through the noise of the storm? Only a few minutes ago getting across the ice field was our biggest worry. Now these bloodthirsty wolves might kill us all. Is this my Golgotha?*

A fast-moving cloudbank obscured his view. The mix of ice and snow swirled and danced around him, stinging his face. He stood there motionless, the scar on his forehead throbbing like a fiery flame. *The others may already be dead.*

He dropped to his knees, exhausted, resigned to his fate. He closed his eyes. *I'm ready.* He tried to resign his mind to what was to come.

He felt hot breath on his face. *Now it happens.* He opened one eye just a slit, and was overjoyed to see a large muzzle next to his face. "Tillie!" he hollered. "You followed me back across!" The ox stood over him, waiting obediently for a command.

A voice was yelling in his ear: "Reverend, thank God! Did you bring more bullets for the Henry?" The voice sounded far away, yet next to his ear.

"No! Horse spooked!" he answered. Virgil bent over him, hands cupped around his mouth.

"Are you hurt?"

"'No!" he replied, yelling at the top of his lungs into the storm.

"Get on the sled, Reverend, I'll turn it back around!" Molly's got the rifle! My hands'r near froze. Took my gloves off to reload an' touched the lever. Hand stuck to it! She pulled it free, tryin to reload. Tore the skin! I can't grip it to shoot! Not much good shootin with my other hand neither!"

The sound of Molly firing the Henry cut through the roaring wind. *Boom! Boom! With the echo of each shot mixing in, it was impossible to locate her.*

"They're all around us!"

*Boom!*

"She's fired again!" Donald shouted.

"Cain't see them, but they're there! Colt's got one shot left!. Rev, get the shovel! We'll use it if they attack!"

*Boom!*

"On, Tillie!" Virgil shouted. The ox lunged forward, nearly jerking both men off the sled.

"Molly Mae!" Ricketts shouted. "We can't just leave her!"

The girl suddenly appeared out of the blinding snow, and jumped on the back of the sled, falling onto the two men. "No more bullets! Reverend! What are you doing here?!"

"On, Tillie!" Virgil shouted. The beast surged forward.

"I was looking for the both of you!"

Suddenly, it was dead calm, the only sound from the runners

on the sled as they slid on the ice. The fast-moving storm swept on down the mountain and ended just as quickly as it had started, leaving in its wake a gentle snowfall and a brief appearance of the sun.

They were halfway across the ice field, when a sheer drop-off on either side of the sled loomed ahead. The sure-footed ox was cautiously finding her way, laboring in the thin air. The overloaded sled began digging into the ice, rather than sliding on top of it.

Surreptitious movements caught Ricketts' attention. "Do you see them?!" he yelled.

"There! Just inside the tree line! There are more than a dozen!" Molly Mae shrieked. "Oh, no!"

Virgil got off the sled, barely able to gain footing on the uneven, slippery ice. Hooking his arm through Tillie's harness, he worked his way forward until he was ahead of the ox. *Gotta lead her across. Gotta get her to go faster.* "On, Tillie, on, Tillie!" He tugged at the yoke. The ox leaned forward but could not budge the sled, its runners frozen in place. All three began yelling at the ox: "On, Tillie! On, Tillie!"

"Here they come!" the reverend yelled.

The pack of wolves started across the ice field toward them; the big male leader a few steps ahead of the others. They covered the distance in seconds.

"Get behind me!" Ricketts roared. He stood up to face the lead wolf. He raised the shovel over his head and swung it menacingly, directly in the face of the wolf who was just a few feet away.

A deafening volley of shots rang out from the nearby trees on the far end of the narrow ridge. *Boom, boom, itdy, boom, boom!* Three of the wolves dropped in their tracks, but the leader of the pack was still standing. Startled, it stopped to sniff the air. A second volley rang out in rapid succession: *Boom, boom, itdy, boom, boom!* Hit by multiple bullets, the big male dropped, its head landing on the back of the sled. The loss of their leader and the resounding echoes from the muzzle blasts were sufficient for the remaining members of the pack to hastily retreat to the safety of the tree line.

Howard Stall stepped out into view. He walked carefully toward the trio, followed by Willard Clark and several other men.

Virgil held up his hand to stop them. "Wait, it's too slippery! We'll come to y'all."

"Not bad shootin'," Stall yelled at the trio. "Must be eighty yards or more." He waved back. "Get on over here, then, so we can take a look at all y'all. I don't think they'll be back. We got the leader."

"Sled's locked in the ice, we were sittin' ducks!" Virgil yelled.

"Hold on; we'll throw you a rope," Willard offered.

That afternoon, wrapped in blankets and sitting on wood rounds that circled a large fire, the trio revisited their encounter with the wolves. When it was the reverend's turn to talk about his adventures, he included his earlier encounter with the wolves. Stall listened intently.

"That's a good one, Rev! Next time I'm surrounded by wolves, I'll yell 'bang!'" Stall chortled, slapping his knee. "I'll have to try that." His laughter was infectious.

Virgil shook his head and grinned at Molly Mae, whom, he had discovered, was quite good at nursing his raw, frostbitten fingers.

"Wagons are bunched up a mile or so that-a-way at the Laurel Hill," Stall said. "After a coupla broken axles, nobody's in a hurry now. Had lotsa volunteers to backtrack and find you. We're gonna need all the muscle we kin get. Wagons hafta be let down one at a time through the chutes, or they slide all the way down across the Devil's Backbone into th' Sandy River! Never seen so many latecomers that never seen snow. Might take a week or more to get ever'body down, iffen the ropes hold up. Will ya please pass me s'more of them vittles? You're a fine cook, young lady. Better'n mountain cat or stewed wolf."

"Thank you, sir." Molly Mae curtsied gracefully, a wide smile dimpling her cheeks.

Everyone held plates up for more of the vegetable stew and roasted beef from the Dutch oven. The cooking pot and food were gifts from a group of miners heading east, eager for information about the road ahead. They were especially interested in how the group had crossed the ice field.

Stall got up, and refilled coffee cups all around. The pewter cups, belonging to Phyllis Clark, made perfect hand warmers. He noticed the reverend's Henry rifle that now leaned against a nearby tree. Virgil had returned the second Colt to him. He patted the holster, and queried: "Why'd you cross back over, Rev? You didn't have your rifle, 'n you was safe, anyways, nearly across the ice. We was a-watchin' you. B'sides, ya didn't have no gun, an' no bullets."

Ricketts looked thoughtful. "Molly Mae here was in my keep. Thought I could save her, even if I couldn't save her man there, Mister Verin Palmer."

"Reverend!" Molly Mae flushed with embarrassment. Stall seemed not to hear. He wanted more of the story.

"We was yelling at you to keep comin' our way, but you started back across—bravest thing I ever did see," Stall said, continuing. He clapped Donald on the back, yet again. "It was the storm, I guess, you couldn't no way hear us after yore horse runned off. Changed what we was a-seein' from the trees. Bravest thing, you standin' on that sled like ya did, a-swingin' that …" He paused in mid-sentence: "Mind if I see yore shovel, Rev?"

"It ain't ours. It's yours, from th' station," Virgil said. He walked over to the Clark's wagon and retrieved the shovel.

Stall took it as gently as if he were handling a baby. He looked it up and down, rubbing his bare hand slowly across the metal surface from the step to the blade to the tip. The others looked at him with curiosity, puzzled at his sudden interest.

"Hit's mine fer shore," he said finally. "If them two was already dead…" he paused again, slowly turning the shovel over to expose the back side while he continued to inspect it. "Then… you'd a-walked right into them wolves fer shore, bare-handed."

"I had to do something. Maybe you'da done it different. Maybe I thought God would bind up the mouths of the wolves like Daniel in the Lion's den." He corrected himself. "No. That wasn't it. The mountain took us all down to bare metal. I knew I had nothing to fight them wolves with."

There was silence around the fire. It snapped and popped as Willard added more wood. A cascade of sparks rose skyward. More snow fell from the nearby trees with a *whump!* Stall nodded, watching the tiny embers fly in all directions. He seemed reluctant to turn loose of the shovel. Finally, he passed it to Willard Clark.

"But you did find somethin' to fight with! Rev'rend, me and Mister Clark here, we saw you swingin' somethin' different over your head at them wolves."

Virgil and Molly Mae looked from one man to the other, unable to follow the gist of the exchange. "Just what in tarnation you talkin' about?" Virgil exclaimed impatiently.

"Looked like a sword of some kind, not a shovel. A long sword. The sun reflecting off the snow, maybe."

"No mistaking it," Willard Clark added. "It looked to both of us like it was on fire, too."

Reverend Ricketts looked stunned, and stammered: "Sword of the Spirit?" *But it was only a borrowed shovel.*

"Me," Stall stated, "I'da not never tried it without a rifle with a full load in both six-guns, a knife, an' a passel o' extra bullets. Bravest thing I ever seen, I do believe," he said again. "A man takes on a dozen wolves with nothin' but a shovel." He shook his head in disbelief. "You had nothin' when you started back across, then ya had a flaming sword when we seen you again. It don't make no human sense.

"Somefin' to tell yore kids about, little lady, I reckon. He's a-shinin' on y'all, Rev'rend." Stall was looking skyward. "From somewhere up there, he's a-shinin' on all three of y'all. Mister Clark, you give that shovel back to the Rev now. My bestest gift to ya, an' take good care of it."

After the others had headed for the warmth of their bedrolls, Virgil and Molly Mae sat by the dying embers of the fire. "I'll be staying in the Clark's wagon tonight," she said. "I don't know who's driving down the chutes in the morning. Maybe Mister Stall. We're first in line now, they're letting us go first because of what we've been through. The Clarks expect you'll come with us, and Reverend Ricketts, too. But that's up to you. Mister Stall plans to tie on to the back of our wagon and loop around a tree to slow it down; says he's done it before. Most of the ropes have been used up, and we don't have time to make more out of rawhide. So, I wanted to give you something, in case you don't come, since I'm leaving in the morning with the Clarks. Something for you to remember Claire by."

He turned and looked at her. "What? We got nothin' left."

She removed a small canvas sack from her apron and held it out to Virgil. He tried to open it, but his hands refused to cooperate.

"Here, let me help you." Inside was a seedling pine tree, its roots buried in a small clump of dirt. "I dug it near her grave. Since she didn't want you to go back there, I thought..." Her words fell away as she saw tears streaming down Virgil's cheeks. "Is it the wrong thing?" She stood up, embarrassed that she had brought him to tears. "Plant it wherever you end up." She turned to walk away.

"Molly Mae," he called, "I cain't get over Claire right away. We was the same as married an' all. We had plans. I was gonna build a cabin in the woods, she was gonna keep house, plant a garden."

"Everybody had plans before they got here, even Mister Stall. I had plans too, you know? Plans change. People change. My father and me were gonna start boating on the Columbia, like we did back home. Helping folks get from The Dalles to Fort Vancouver or Portland town. I don't think that will ever happen. Maybe the mountain does that, makes us see that sometimes even what we think are the best plans just don't work out. We nearly died back there. It has to have been for something. I want to see the whole valley now, before I settle anywhere."

"I'd like that, too," Virgil muttered.

"Willard and Phyllis are going south down the valley. Got to be warmer weather somewhere south of here, don't you think? A better place to settle, maybe?" She stood still, waiting for him to respond, hoping to somehow prolong what she feared would be their last chance to talk.

He mumbled noncommittally, so she turned to walk away.

"Molly Mae!" he called after her again. "If I walk alongside the Clark's wagon, a-travelin' south, we c'd go on. You an' me. I mean, to th' end o' th' valley. We c'd see what's there, mebbe?"

"You can be free of me in the morning, Virgil. You have to make up your own mind. No matter what Claire asked of you, I'm not one to insist on what others want for me. You shouldn't rest on that either. Especially when she's not...not with us anymore."

She walked toward the Clark's wagon. Ghostly shadows sprang from the embers in the dying firelight, making her petite body look wraithlike. *Makes her look taller, like she's floatin' away,* Virgil thought, realizing he was smiling in spite of himself, *but she's alive, like me.*

He laid down next to the waning fire, rolled up in a blanket, but he was unable to sleep. He arose at midnight and threw the last of the nearby pieces of wood on the fire. Sparks rose, and the damp wood sizzled and popped as pitch pockets erupted, each causing brief bursts of crackling hot blue-red flames. The fire came back to life and illuminated the surrounding area. He removed Claire's sketchbook from his shirt and thumbed through the pages.

She had written a note to herself inside the front cover, and he read it aloud: "I'm going to make my own way now." He looked up and caught sight of Molly Mae. She was standing outside the Clark's wagon, a shawl around her shoulders, shivering with cold.

"Molly Mae? Why ain't you in bed? Y'all wanta catch yer death o' cold?!"

"Both the Clarks snore something awful," she replied, walking back to warm herself by the fire.

"I been sittin' here thinkin.' Uncle Stubbs told me 'bout a place down south. Skinner's Mud Hole, he calls it."

"It doesn't sound like much to me," she replied. "Is there a river there?"

"Two big ones. They come t'gether north of town. Howard told me. He's been there. I'm gonna head there. I'll find a place to plant Claire's tree. Gotta be some place high up. Mebbe high enough t' see Mount Hood. I think Claire'd like it, if..."

"If what?" she asked.

A rush of tenderness softened his voice to a whisper: "If *you* were there."

She drew a little closer to him, and he timidly and carefully wrapped his blanket around her shivering shoulders. Cautiously, she snuggled closer, looked up, and studied his lean face. "We could work on a lot of things together."

Passage through the narrow Laurel Hill chutes went off smoothly, with Stall directing the descent. They found Number Four Station abandoned, as they expected.

Atop the narrow ridge above the Sandy River, the place called The Devil's Backbone, they could finally see the Willamette Valley for the first time. Rather than stop to enjoy the view, though, Stall insisted they keep going until they made the final descent past Toll Station Number Five and on into Oregon City.

Passage across the narrow ridge was accomplished without major difficulty. Despite Stall's insistence that they keep moving, three people stood together and looked back across the Devil's Backbone, each wondering why it had such a sinister-sounding name.

"We've crossed worse," Virgil stated. "Mebbe at the end of th' road, all the meanness we ever had is gone 'cept the backbone—the meat's picked clean. Mebbe from here on it gits better. We all come fer somethin' better."

"Somebody at this end must have named it," Reverend Ricketts added. "Maybe they knew it wasn't the most dangerous part of the road. Maybe, the greed in folks shows up again once they get here, like the devil's looking down on us. Everything has a price for them willing to pay. Here, now, we're standing on top of it, we beat it down. Down there, who knows. We'll find out soon enough if we did right by coming here."

"Molly Mae. What d' you think made th' name?" Virgil asked.

"I think it was supposed to scare folks from leaving, going back over the road the other way. Everything about Oregon scared me until I got here. Now, there's nothing back that way for me. We've paid our dues, all of us, to get here. Everything we left behind is on the other side of the Devil's Backbone. We have a new chance to get it right in the Willamette Valley." She glanced at Virgil.

Howard Stall and Willard Clark were already scouting the road ahead. Phyllis drove the wagon close behind. They did not look back.

The trio hurried to catch up. After another mile, they were out of the snow. At the small town of Rhododendron, they arrived at the final toll station, Number Five. The toll keeper was as surprised to see Howard Stall as he was to see the weary travelers. He stumbled over himself with hospitality.

Once hot coffee, fresh bread and preserves had been served all around, Stall strolled over to him and handed the toll keeper his metal can of tokens, given to travelers who had paid the toll. "I won't be needin' these anymore," he said.

"You givin' up Number Three Station?

"Yup," Stall answered. "Railroad's done finished t' San Francisco. A Creole man c'd live on that train, he'p folks movin' east 'n west. Just like Station Three, only with a change o' scene ever' day, an' no wolves. Now, that's livin'!"

"But it ain't pushed North yet," the toll keeper replied.

"Be here soon enough, I reckon."

**The End**

# Epilogue

"HERE," VERIN ANNOUNCED. "I THINK SHE'D LIKE THIS SPOT." They stood together among the young firs on the east side of Spencer Butte. "Has a good view of th' valley. On a clear day, mebbe we c'n even see Mount Hood."

"Will there be enough room here among the other bushes and trees?" she asked.

"Pine trees grow fast. It'll catch up, 'less th' yew wood an' maples crowd it out." He dug in silence. Molly Mae watched as he carefully placed the sketchbook in the bottom of the hole and planted the tree on top of it. "There," he finally said, patting the ground gently. "Finished."

"If you plan to settle here, you can come as often as you like and pull the grass away," she suggested.

Verin was thinking about something else. "Willard don't like livin' among so many people here. He an' Phyllis are goin' further west in th' morning. There's a trail north o' town, an' they're gonna foller it. I ain't sure they'll ever be satisfied 'til they see the ocean. The rev' is taggin' along. He heard there're still some Indians in th' Coast Range somewhere. He wants to be a farmer now, too. He says there's a li'l valley out that way. Good water. Lotsa grass, tall trees all around. Some people livin' there, not many. Lotsa room."

"What about Tillie?"

"The rev' wanted t' buy Tillie fer five dollars an' use 'er to pull a plow. He thinks he c'n hire out th' both o' them for spring plantin'."

"A man can grow just about anything in this country, even if all he has is a shovel to start out. He should wait until he's settled to take on an animal to take care of," she replied.

"I just let 'im have 'er. Not sure I c'd put a price on somethin' that weren't never really mine. He did say if I ever wanted Tillie back, th' only thing he'd take in trade was a banjo. Funny thing, don'cha think?"

"Funny thing, for sure," Molly Mae replied. "Do you think we'll ever see Mister Stall again?"

"Don't reckon so. He's changed his mind again. Gonna rejoin th' army now. Said he weren't never paid whenever he was in Andersonville durin' th' war. He figgers t' bargain fer his back pay iffen they want him t' re-enlist. Tired of th' snow, I reckon."

He reached for her hand, and she took it cautiously. She had nursed his raw fingers for weeks, applying grease, oatmeal paste, and whatever else she could find that might help them heal. "How do they feel?"

"Feelin' comin' back from th' frostbite."

Verin decided the moment had come to voice the thoughts that had been brewing inside him from the first day they had arrived in Eugene City. He realized he no longer felt as if he was betraying Claire. He knew he was ready to face the future, and that he wanted Molly Mae to be a part of his.

"Stay with me," he proposed shyly, yet firmly. "I always liked th' name Elizabeth. Could y' warm to it?"

She looked up at him and smiled.

"Mebbe the Clarks'll find what they're looking for in that li'l valley. Mebbe you 'n me c'n buy some land fer our own one day. I'll build us a cabin and learn t' grow things. We c'n visit th' Rev' an' Tillie anytime we want. An' you c'n help me with m' letters an' numbers."

"I'd like to do all those things," she said.

Verin felt the weight of the watch that Claire had given him in the pocket of his overalls. *Always my angel,* he thought to himself. He smiled and gently squeezed Elizabeth's hand.

# Final note from the author

IN 1921 THE UNITED STATES BEGAN TO HONOR THOSE WHO GAVE both their lives and their identities in war with a solitary catch-all monument: the Tomb of the Unknowns in Arlington National Cemetery. A solitary honor guard soldier watches over those remains day and night. Interestingly, the remains of the serviceman selected to represent the 'unknowns' of the Vietnam war was later identified through advances in mitochondrial DNA testing, and was moved back to his home town.

The germ that sprouted into *The Angel's Backbone* began with visits to the grave of the unknown pioneer woman buried along the east fork of the Salmon River near the junction of Mount Hood Highway 35 and U.S. Highway 26. She died in 1847, much earlier than the woman in this story.

That she be an immigrant, and that she demonstrate the grit of those women who traveled the Oregon Trail alone was important to me. Mystery surrounds the unknown pioneer woman buried along the trail, and I sought to solve it in my own way. The truth may be much different; however, the goodness, hopes, and dreams my heroine expressed in the midst of personal tragedy was probably typical of the times in which she lived.

The reader might conclude that the high Cascade Mountains themselves, rugged, snowcapped, rising like a spine above the clouds, gave the book its title, but for Claire O'Connor, for whom there is no honor guard, the angels guard her bones.

As a people, we continue to accept risks as we journey farther into space. Upon arrival in other worlds, travelers will no doubt reflect with pride that not all ventures are powered by greed. Like an itch on the bottom of a foot, we are driven to go forth to soothe that itch, to push beyond what was once impossible.

For me, it was the same for the early pioneers, our ancestors, who knew and endured the risks, in order to accomplish even bigger dreams than they could imagine.

DAVID C. HASCALL

# Acknowledgments

A SPECIAL THANK YOU TO MY EDITOR, MEG GRAF, WHO WORKED
tirelessly to give Virgil Stubbs (AKA Verin Palmer) his unique voice.
Your thoughtful suggestions found their way onto page after page.
My hearfelt thanks to:

Research assistant, John O'Donoghue, for his assistance in
locating a suitable topographical map of Mount Hood.

Drivers Dennis Westfall, Dennis Gardner, and Jeff Moses, for
sharing the driving while the four amigos explored portions of
the Oregon Trail, the National Historic Oregon Trail Interpretive
Center in Baker City, and portions of the Barlow Road.

Fellow explorer, wife and my best friend, Barbara, for exploring
even more of the road with me.

Proofreaders, Trish Hascall and Laurie Miller.

Interior artist, Vicki Cox, who drew the two pictures for the
interior of The Angel's Backbone

Together, we made Verin Palmer and the others into real people
and told their story as I believe they would want it to be told.